DEDALUS EUROPEAN CLASSICS

The Dark Domain

Stefan Grabinski

The Dark Domain

Translated with an introduction by
Miroslaw Lipinski
and an afterword by Madeleine Johnson

Dedalus/Hippocrene

Supported by the Eastern Arts Board

Published in the UK by Dedalus Ltd, Langford Lodge, St Judith's Lane, Sawtry, Cambs, PE17 5XE

UK ISBN 1 873982 25 9

Published in the USA by Hippocrene Books Inc, 171, Madison Avenue, New York, NY10016

US ISBN 0 7818 0211 3

Distributed in Canada by Marginal Distribution, Unit 103, 277, George Street North, Ontario, KJ9 3G9

Distributed in Australia & New Zealand by Peribo Pty Ltd, 26, Tepko Road, Terrey Hills, N.S.W. 2084

Publishing History
First published in Poland 1918/22
First English edition 1993

Translation & Introduction copyright © Miroslaw Lipinski 1993
Afterword copyright © Madeleine Johnston 1993

Typeset by Datix International Limited, Bungay, Suffolk, NR35 1EF
Printed in Finland by Wsoy

Contents

INTRODUCTION

Though he wrote a vast quantity of some of the most original and interesting fantastic and bizarre fiction of the 20th Century, Stefan Grabinski remained during his lifetime a generally neglected figure in Poland and, except for two insignificant appearances in Italy, untranslated. His greatest successes occurred between the years 1918 and 1922, when five collections of his stories were published. This impressive output did little, however, to make Grabinski's work accepted in a country that didn't take supernatural fiction seriously. Grabinski did not court critics and the public, and quickly developed a combative stance in regard to criticism of his writings. It is not surprising – and it is most revealing – that in one of his earliest stories, 'The Area,' he formulated his fictional counterpart: the dedicated artist who disdains the normal and separates himself from the public while advancing toward a realization of powerful, supernatural forces born of his own imagination. Like the character in this story, Grabinski was an idealistic loner who strove for an understanding of the hidden forces of both the world and the human mind, and whose creative integrity depended upon representing those forces in the most potent framework available – in Grabinski's case, supernatural fiction.

Grabinski was born in Kamionka Strumilowa, a town near Lwow, on February 26, 1887. The son of a district judge, he suffered from ill-health and developed tuberculosis of the bone at an early age. His sickly nature, coupled with a dreamy, introspective disposition, undoubtedly led to his involvement with fantastic fiction. In 1909 he self-published a small volume of macabre writings that disappeared as most self-published efforts do. Forced by necessity, he became a teacher in secondary school, but his literary aspirations did not abate. He continued writing and, after the disruption of the First World War, made his

7

'official debut' in 1918 with the six-story collection *On the Hill of Roses*. This volume – which included the Grabinski classic, 'Strabismus' – drew some fine reviews. Most impressed was Karol Irzykowski, an important critic and an author of innovative avant-garde fiction. Irzykowski, already familiar with a couple of Grabinski's stories that had appeared in the respected journal *Maski*, proclaimed the author as strikingly original, someone who exhibited a keen intelligence and a masterful style – an extraordinary phenomenon in a country whose writers generally remained, because of the country's tragic history, concerned with 'Polish issues.'

Indeed, nowhere in Polish literature, before or since, has there been an author who excelled in supernatural fiction as Grabinski did and who devoted himself so singularly to that one genre.

While Grabinski proved he could write a straightforward chiller like 'A Tale of the Gravedigger,' most of his best work is open to multi-layered interpretation and involves a compendium of influences, both old and new, as it presents a coherent Grabinski-esque world view. A vigorous opponent of mechanism and determinism, he integrated the concepts of such ancient philosophers as Heraclitus and Plato with the contemporary philosophies of Henri Bergson and Maurice Maeterlinck in his battle against a modern world where man's primordial sense of self and nature was being erased by machine, restrictive systems and people of little vision.

Bergson was a particularly important influence. Grabinski used his theory of durational time to splendid effect in 'Saturnin Sektor.' But it was Bergson's concept of *élan vital* – that spiritual force, or energy, that underlies reality and influences matter – which struck the deepest cord in Grabinski. He merged this 'vital force' with theories of motion, advanced by scientists like Newton and Einstein, in a group of train stories, collected under the title *The Motion Demon* in 1919.

Undoubtedly because of the importance of train travel,

The Motion Demon collection found the warmest reception of all of Grabinski's books in Poland. It is easy to picture a train traveller reading with fascination and unease these tales of maverick railwaymen, insane passengers and mysterious trains. But Grabinski was not merely interested in entertaining the populace. The train world provided Grabinski with a perfect symbol for Bergson's *élan vital*. Here was a forward-moving force, powerful, direct, one that could be felt under one's feet and in the motions of the car, a force that could easily represent the hidden force of life; here was a milieu that every person of those times could understand. The train world was a direct conduit to the primary issues of Grabinski's own anti-authoritarian, anti-materialistic world view.

Grabinski certainly did not shy away from another of life's integral 'forces' − sex. While matters sexual were being investigated in the psychoanalytic debates of the day, Grabinski used his fiction to reveal, with frank boldness, the dark forces of the libido in such tales as 'Fumes,' 'Szamota's Mistress' and 'In the Compartment.' In a couple of these tales Grabinski anticipated the issue of gender identity, so topical nowadays. Several of his train stories end with obvious orgiastic explosions, and 'Szamota's Mistress' may be, on one level, a unique tale of masturbation-induced frenzy.

Atypically for one raised in a non-Western culture, Grabinski tended to stay away from using the rich Polish folklore tradition available to him. In this sense, his eyes were turned toward the West rather than the East; he took a modern approach to fantastic literature. When he did borrow supernatural entities for his fiction, they were known to the folklore of all European cultures. Yet even these entities became distinctly Grabinski-esque. In 'Vengeance of the Elementals' he used those malicious beings that influence and hover around the elements (in this case, fire elementals), and made them combatants in his own philosophical fight − besides giving them some amusing, and highly original, names. (Fire, of course, represented another basic 'force' that modern man was naively becoming less aware of and, hence, concerned about; which is why Grabinski also wrote of series of 'fire stories,' collected in *The Book of Fire* in 1922.)

All of Grabinski's innovative tales were examples of a particular type of fantasy, which he proposed calling 'psychofantasy' or 'metafantasy.' As opposed to straightforward, conventional fantasy that displayed the outward and the ornamental, this type of fantasy employed as its basis psychological, philosophical or metaphysical concerns. The author, in effect, was a studious magus who would uncover the hidden, and maybe not explain 'the dark domain,' for that was something the mind could never do, but acknowledge its presence and treat it with psychic respect.

When Grabinski began to abandon, for the most part, the short story format around 1922 and turn to novel writing, his self-motivated calling as a serious investigator of the unknown flowered into mysticism, a circumstance that doomed his work in the eyes of the critics. Grabinski began taking far less of an intellectual stance in his writings, and his wicked humour, evident in many of his short stories, lessened and ultimately disappeared.

Not unexpectedly, his novels were not well received by the public. Grabinski, however, stayed his course and did not abandon the literature he felt could convey life as he saw it.

Yet his body would not let him wage his literary battle with full physical strength. In 1929 his tuberculosis spread to his lungs, with resultant hemorrhaging, making teaching an impossibility. For health reasons he was forced to move to the country. His situation quickly became desperate. Medicines and proper care were costly, as was his new secluded residence. Aware of his pitiful situation, Karol Irzykowski and another critic, Jerzy Plomienski, succeeded in getting the city of Lwow to acknowledge its native son. Grabinski was given the Lwow Literary Award in 1931, but the money he received was soon dissipated, impelling him to give up the country retreat and move back to Lwow.

Grabinski's last years were torturous. Restricted mostly to his bed, barely able to write yet never giving up, he withered away, his mother by his side. Jerzy Plomienski visited the author at the end of 1935, when Grabinski was completely bedridden. Plomienski found the author transformed beyond all recognition by his illness, the once noble features gone, the face ashen and bearded, the eyes glassy, the lips swollen and chapped and allowing the escape of blood-tinged saliva. Plomienski tried his best to bolster the dying author's spirits, telling him that his works were destined to be read and acknowledged in future generations, that he would find acclaim abroad. Grabinski refused to be swayed and bitterly complained that writers who wanted to be individuals and not followers of literary fashion had no place in Poland.

On November 12, 1936 Grabinski finally died. There were a few notices and a couple of touching tributes in newspapers and journals by those, like Irzykowski, who knew him and recognized the value of his work. Then the Second World War clothed everything in its dark pall, and it seemed that Grabinski would never be heard of again.

Yet, beginning in 1949, Grabinski's work saw a revival in Poland. That year an important collection of Polish fantasy, edited by the poet Julian Tuwim, contained two Grabinski stories. Later on, in the 1950s, a collection of Grabinski's best work was published, as well as a mammoth thesis by Professor Artur Hutnikiewicz devoted to Grabinski's *oeuvre*. It is possible that some of Poland's young, rebellious filmmakers became familiar with the misanthropic author, notably Roman Polanski, whose films *Repulsion* and *The Tenant* share certain Grabinski trademarks. (*The Tenant*, though based on a French novel by Roland Topor, is disconcertingly filled with many Grabinski-isms.) Gradually more of Grabinski's work was published, including a collection in 1975 edited by the famous SF writer Stanislaw Lem, one of Grabinski's strongest admirers. The 1980s saw Grabinski's work translated into German, including two volumes published under the 'Library of the

House of Usher' imprint, and Grabinski's name appeared alongside those of Blackwood, Lovecraft and Machen.

And now this maverick of the macabre who wrote in spiritual seclusion and in physical pain, who wrote consumed with the essence of the dark domain, is before a new audience.

It is impossible to know what Grabinski felt in the final moments of his life. Surely there must have been despair, anger, bitterness, and perhaps even resignation. But if he reflected on a central tenet in his tales – that no thought disappears, that one day it will be made flesh – then maybe he would have, as he breathed his last, hoped for a genuine revival and validation of his work in the future. It is this thought, this hope, that has been indeed made flesh. One of the great voices of supernatural fiction lives again.

Miroslaw Lipinski

FUMES

A new herd of gusts advanced from the ravines, and set loose over snow-covered fields, they ploughed their enraged heads through the snowbanks. Raised from its soft bedding, the snow whirled in huge cyclones, bottomless funnels, slender whips, and, wrapping itself up in a hundred-fold repeated whirlpool, sprayed out white, granular powder.

An early winter evening was coming on.

The blindingly white blizzard gradually changed to a bluish hue, the pearl-grey horizon turned a morose black. The snow fell continuously. Large, shaggy strands silently glided from somewhere above and layered the ground. Hay-like stacks rose up; a hundred white caps piled on top of each other. Snowy anthills, light like down, moved rhythmically with the wind, creating a pattern of slanting ridges. Where it blew stronger, precipitous snowdrifts swelled to a height of three peasants. Where the wind's caustic tongue scraped everything up, an open, clod-frozen earth appeared.

Slowly the wind alleviated, and furling its tired wings, it warbled softly somewhere in the valley. The landscape settled and solidified in the night frost . . . .

Ozarski worked his way tirelessly down the middle of the road. Covered in a hooded greatcoat, wearing thick, knee-high boots, loaded down with surveying equipment, the young engineer moved with difficulty through the piles of snow blocking his way. Two hours ago, blinded by the snowstorm, he had become separated from his colleagues and lost in a vast field, and after wandering without success in every direction, he had set off along this road. Now, seeing the rapidly descending evening, he exerted all his strength so that he could arrive at a village and put in somewhere for the night before complete darkness set in. But the road dragged on endlessly, empty and barren, its sides unrelieved by even a poor hut or a wayside smithy. An uncomfortable feeling of isolation gripped him. He momentarily removed his sweat-moistened fur cap and, while wiping its inside with a handkerchief, drew breath into his weary chest.

He went on. The road gradually changed its course and, bending widely, fell to the west. After rounding a prominent crag, the engineer started to descend into the valley with a quickened step. Suddenly, as he was rapidly scanning the area before him with his grey, sharp-sighted eyes, he let out an involuntary cry of joy. Down at the bottom of the road, on the right-hand side, flickered a dim little light: he was within reach of a human habitation. He hastened his step and, after a fifteen-minute vigorous hike, stood before a shoddy, snow-covered structure. It was a type of roadside inn without outbuildings, without a stable – part house, part hut – erected in complete seclusion. All about, as far as the eye could see, there was no sign of any village, farmsteads or settlements; just a couple of unleashed snow flurries kept on barking in furious yelps, like guard dogs, over the lonely habitation . . . .

He knocked on the rotting door. It immediately burst open, and at the entrance to a dimly-lit hallway he was greeted by an athletically-built, white-haired man with a peculiarly hopeful smile. Ozarski, closing the door behind himself, bowed slightly to the landlord and asked for a night's lodging. The old man nodded his head amicably and, taking in with an exploratory glance the healthy, firm figure of the young man, said in a voice to which he tried to impart a possibly gentle, even tender, tone:

'There will be a place – oh, yes; there will be a place to lay down your bright little head. And I won't be stingy with food; I'll feed you and give you something to drink; yes, yes; I'll give you something to drink. Only why don't you come closer, sir, here into the room; it'll be nice and warm.'

And with a gentle, protective movement, he encircled him about the waist and led him to the open doorway of the room. This seemed too familiar to Ozarski, and he would have gladly freed himself. But the old man's arm held him firmly about the middle, and whether he liked it or not he had to accept this peculiar cordiality from the innkeeper.

While crossing the high threshold with some hesitancy, Ozarski suddenly stumbled and lost his balance. He would have fallen had it not been for the willing help of his companion, who held onto him and, raising him like a child, carried him effortlessly into the room. Here, gently placing him on the ground, the old man said in a strangely altered voice:

'Well, sir, how was it travelling through the air? You're as light as a feather.'

Ozarski looked with amazement at the white-haired giant who had thought him, a man tall and well-built, as light as a feather. He was impressed by his strength, yet at the same time he couldn't fight off a particular impression of distaste created by the innkeeper's inappropriate familiarity and intrusive warmth. Now, in the glare of a simple kitchen lamp hanging on a rope from a filthy ceiling, Ozarski could get a thorough look at him. He was maybe seventy years old, but the healthy, vigorous posture and the recent display of strength, unusual for this age, disorientated the observer. The big face, covered with warts, was framed on both sides by long, silvery white hair cut evenly near the shoulders. Most interesting of all were the old man's eyes. Black, of demonic glitter, they burned with wild, lecherous fire. The same look was betrayed by a wide face with a strong, prominent jaw and fat, sensuous lips. For Ozarski the impression was, on the whole, unpleasant and instinctively repellent, though he couldn't resist a certain magnetic effect exerted by the fascinating eyes.

Meanwhile, the old man busied himself with supper. He took down from a shelf some smoked bacon and a loaf of whole-wheat bread, he drew out from a green cupboard a demijohn of vodka, and placed everything on the table before his guest.

15

'Eat, sir, eat. Don't spare yourself anything. I'll bring you some hot borsch right away.'

He then patted Ozarski familiarly on the knee and immediately disappeared behind the door to a neighbouring room.

As he ate, Ozarski glanced about the room. It was low, square, with a heavily smoke-stained ceiling. In one corner, near the window, stood a bed or a bed of boards, opposite it – a type of counter with barrels and a small cask of beer. The place was filthy. Cobwebs, uncleared for years, spread out their grey, monotonous threads over the ceiling and a stack of coal.

'A dive,' he muttered through his teeth.

Close to the entrance door, a fire blazed under a stove; higher up, coals were dying out in a baker's oven, over which was a wide square hood. The softly smouldering embers merged with the bubbling food cooking on the stove into some mysterious, drowsy chat, into a muffled murmur of a humid interior set against the background of the riotous snowstorm outside.

The door to the other room squeaked, and, contrary to Ozarski's expectation, a stocky girl hastened to the stove. She removed the large stone pot from the fire and, tilting it, poured its contents into a deep clay bowl. The borsch was hearty and thick. The girl silently placed the fragrant soup in front of Ozarski, while with the other hand she gave him a tin spoon from a cabinet. As she did this, she leaned over so close to him, that one of her breasts, hanging out freely from her blouse, brushed his cheek. The engineer trembled. The breast was firm and young.

The girl drew back, and sitting down near him on a bench, wordlessly fixed her large, blue, almost watery eyes on him. She looked twenty, at most. Her luxuriant golden-red hair fell down to her shoulders in two thick braids; the top of her hair was parted evenly, like a village beauty's. The rather good-looking face was disfigured by a lengthy scar that, starting at the middle of the forehead, cut through the left eyebrow. The generously-developed breasts, which she didn't attempt to cover at all with the border of her blouse, had the hue of pale-yellow marble and were overgrown with a light, golden down. On the right breast was a birthmark shaped like a horseshoe.

He liked her. He reached out his hand for her breasts, which he started to stroke. She didn't defend herself and sat in silence.

'What's your name?'

'Makryna.'

'A beautiful name. Is that your father in there?'

And he gestured with his hand toward the closed room where the old man had disappeared.

The girl smiled mysteriously.

'Who? In there? There's no one there now.'

'Come, come! Don't evade the question. The innkeeper, the owner of this place, that's who I mean. Are you his daughter or his lover?'

'Not one or the other!' she burst out with a deep, hearty laugh.

'So you're just a servant girl?'

She clouded up proudly.

'Humph! So that is what you think! I'm the landlady here.'

Ozarski was astounded.

'Well, then, he's your husband?'

Makryna shook with a renewed drawn-out, generous laugh.

'You haven't guessed it. I'm no one's wife.'

'But you sleep with him, eh? Even though he's lived long, he's still strong. He could take care of three like me. And sparks are constantly flying from his eyes. An old wolf.'

A vague smile appeared on Makryna's crimson lips. She nudged him with her elbow:

'How curious you are! No – I do not sleep with him; no, I don't. How could I? After all, it's from him that I'm – ' She broke off, as if not knowing the appropriate word or as if unable to properly clarify things for him.

All of a sudden, apparently to evade further questions, she slipped free from his already too insistent hands and disappeared into the other room.

'A strange girl.'

He drank down his fifth cup of vodka and, resting his legs comfortably on the bench, leaned back into the chair. A light languor came over him. The excessive warmth of the heated room, his weariness after a long tramp through the snowstorm, and the strong drink – all disposed him to sleepiness. And he would probably have fallen asleep, if not for the re-entrance of the old man. The innkeeper carried under his arm two bottles of wine, and filling glasses for his guest and himself, he said to Ozarski, smacking his lips loudly:

'A superior Hungarian vintage. Why don't you try it? It's older than I am.'

Ozarski mechanically tossed it down. He felt dizzy. The old man was looking at him warmly, from the corner of his eye:

'Ah, that's because you haven't eaten enough, sir. And it'll do you good for the night . . . .'

The engineer didn't understand.

'For the night? What do you mean?'

'Ah, nothing, nothing,' the other dismissed quickly. 'My, you've got strong legs, sir.'

And he pinched his thigh.

Ozarski abruptly drew back, pushing the chair with him. At the same time he searched in his pocket for the revolver that was constantly with him during long expeditions.

The old man leered slimily with his eyes, and said in a surprised voice:

'Sir, why do you jump up from your chair? It's just a simple joke, nothing more. It's just from great friendliness. I've taken a liking to you. Besides, we have a lot of time on our hands.'

And as if to quieten him down, he retreated and leaned his back against the wall.

The engineer composed himself. Wanting to turn the conversation to another, directly opposite track, he asked impudently:

'Where's your girl? Why is she hiding behind that door? Hey, instead of these stupid jokes, bring her to me for the night. I won't pay badly.'

The innkeeper seemed not to understand.

'Pardon me, sir, but I have no girl, and beyond that door there is no one now.'

Ozarski, already well intoxicated, flew into a rage.

'Who are you, old bull, to talk such nonsense right to my face? Where is the girl I had on my knees a moment ago? Call Makryna here, and off with you!'

The giant didn't change his calm position by the wall, but smiling playfully, looked with interest at the irritated man:

'Ah, Makryna, so we're called Makryna today.'

And then ignoring his angry guest, he left with a heavy step to the neighbouring room where the girl had disappeared. Ozarski rushed after him, wanting to force his way inside, but at that moment he saw Makryna coming out.

She was dressed only in her shirt. Her golden-red hair fell in a cascade over her shoulders, a reddish-brassy colour flickering in the light.

In her hands she was holding three baskets full of freshly-kneaded bread. Placing them on a bench nearby, she reached for a pair of tongs and started removing the glowing embers from the oven. Leaning toward the black opening, her figure curved with a strong, firm arch, emphasizing her healthy, maiden shape.

Ozarski forgot himself. He grabbed her in that half-bent position and, raising her shirt, started to cover her flushed body with scorching kisses.

Makryna, laughing, did not interfere. Meanwhile, removing the smouldering firebrands, she carelessly left the rest of the glowing embers along the edges, after which, with the help of a brush, she cleared away the strewn ashes. But the passionate embraces of her guest apparently hindered her too much, for, freeing herself from his arms, she grabbed a shovel and jokingly threatened him with it. Ozarski yielded momentarily, waiting until she would finish with the bread. She proceeded to toss out all the loaves from the basket one right after the other, and sprinkling them one more time with flour, she placed them in the oven. Then she grabbed the oven cover hanging on a string beside her and closed the opening.

The engineer trembled with impatience. Seeing that the work was finished, he advanced predatorily and, pulling her toward the bed, tried to tear off her shirt. But the girl defended herself.

'Not now. It's too early. Later, in about an hour, near midnight, I'll come to take out the bread. Then you will have me. Well, let go now, let go! If I say I'll come, I'll come. I won't let myself be taken by force.'

And with a deft, cat-like movement, she escaped his arms, flitted passed the oven, closed the vent, and disappeared into the neighbouring room. He wanted to force his way inside, but the quickly bolted door wouldn't budge.

'Bitch!' he breathlessly hissed through his teeth. 'But I won't forget about midnight. You have to come out for the loaves. You won't leave them there for the entire night.'

Somewhat calmed by this certainty, he began to undress. He assumed that he wouldn't fall asleep, and so preferred to wait in bed. He put out the lamp and lay down.

The bed was unexpectedly comfortable. He stretched out with delight on the soft bedding, put his hands under his head and surrendered to that particular state before sleep when the mind, wearied from a day's work, half-dreams, floating like a boat entrusted to the waters by a tired oarsman who lets down his hands.

Outside the wind stormed, slashing the windows with snow; farther on, from the woods and fields, and smothered by the sound of the wild wind, came the howl of wolves. Inside, it was warm. The darkness of the interior was brightened only by the weakly glowing embers left behind by Makryna along the sides of the oven. Through the gaps between the cover and the edges of the aperture, the ruby eyes of coals were visible, capturing his attention .... The engineer stared at the dying redness, and dozed. Time lengthened terribly. Every moment he raised his heavy eyelids and, overcoming sleepiness, fixed his eyes at the roving glimmer in the abyss. In his confused thoughts the figures of the lascivious old man and Makryna alternated, by the law of psychic relationship flowing into some strange whole, into some chimerical alloy, brought about by their mutual lasciviousness; their words, odd expressions, their successive appearances unreeled chaotically in a manifest, though not reasonable, arrangement. From covered thickets emerged previously hatched questions, now indolently seeking explanation. Everything loitered about, got entangled along the road, everything jostled sluggishly, sleepily and absurdly ....

An overwhelming stuffiness took possession of his mind, it prevailed in his throat and chest. A dim nightmare managed to slip in .... His impulsively outstretched hand wanted to hold back the enemy, but fettered, it fell back. A stagnant darkness followed ....

At some time during the night Ozarski awoke. He rubbed his eyes lazily, raised his heavy head, and began to listen. He thought he had heard a noise coming from the region of the oven. Indeed, after a moment, a distinct rustling issued from there, like soot giving way in a chimney. He tried to focus his eyes on its cause, but the complete darkness prevented him from doing so.

Suddenly a strip of moonlight penetrated the frosted windows, and cutting the middle of the room with a bright streak, its greenish glow illuminated part of the kitchen.

The engineer instinctively directed his eyes upward, in the direction of the oven, and to his amazement saw a pair of naked, muscular calves dangling from the hood and over the stove. Not changing his position, Ozarski waited with bated breath. Meanwhile, amid the continual noise of falling soot, powerful shanks emerged from the smoke-hole, to be slowly followed by wide, sinewy loins, then a woman's abdomen with strong, expansive lines. Finally, with one jerk, the entire figure came out of the opening and dropped onto the floor. Not far from Ozarski, a huge, horrible hag stood in the moonlight . . . .

She was completely naked, with loosened long white hair falling below her shoulders. Even though, judging by the colour of her hair, she seemed an old woman, her body possessed a strange compactness and flexibility. Entranced, the engineer let his eyes wander along big breasts, firm like a girl's, along strong, solid hips and supple thighs. The hag, as if wanting him to get a more thorough look at her, stood motionless for a long time in the moonlight. After a while she silently advanced toward the bed, pausing in the middle of the room. Now he could clearly see her previously shadow-covered face. He was met by the fiery glance of big black eyes, wildly brilliant against wrinkled eyelids. But he was most amazed by the expression on the face. That old countenance, furrowed by a system of folds and hollows, seemed doubled up. Ozarski sensed in it a familiar physiognomy, but for the present it escaped his mind. Suddenly, realizing where he was, he unraveled the tangled enigma: the hag was looking at him with a double face – the innkeeper's and Makryna's. The repugnant warts spread all over her, the hawk-like nose, the demonic eyes, and the age – belonged to the lecherous old man; on the other hand, the sex (unquestionably a woman's), the white scar from the middle of the forehead to the eyebrow, and especially the birthmark on the right breast – betrayed Makryna.

Shocked by this discovery, he didn't lower his gaze from the hag's magnetic eyes.

Meanwhile, she advanced right up to the bed, and placing one leg along its edge, with the other she rested her big toe on his lips. This happened so unexpectedly that he didn't even have time to avoid the heavy, overpowering foot. He was gripped by a strange fear. In his burdened chest a nervous heart pounded; his lips, pressed down by the toe of the hag, couldn't utter a cry. Thus lasted a long, silent moment.

Slowly the shrew, not changing the position of her legs, removed the quilt and started to take off his underclothes. At first Ozarski attempted to defend himself, but feeling her pressure on him, and his will fettered by the fire of her lustful eyes, he surrendered with some kind of terrible joy.

The hag, noticing the change which had overcome him, removed the foot crushing his lips and, sitting on the bed, began a wild, debauched fondling of his body. After several minutes she gained complete control: he quivered from pleasure. An unleashed heat – animalistic, insatiable, primitive – rocked their bodies and entangled them in a titanic embrace. The lustful female threw herself under his body, and humbly, like a young maiden, drew him into her with a craving movement of her thighs.

Ozarski satisfied her. Then she went crazy. She encircled his middle with her strong arms, ensnared his loins with her muscular legs, and began to squeeze him in a terrific hug. He felt a pain at the small of his back and in his chest.

'Let go! You're strangling me!'

The terrible embrace didn't ease up. He thought she would crush his ribs, shatter his chest. Half-conscious, he laid a free hand on a glittering knife lying on the nearby table, pushed it under her arm, and plunged it in.

A hellish double-cry tore apart the quiet of the night: the savage, animalistic roar of a man – and the sharp, piercing wail of a woman. And then silence, absolute silence . . . .

He felt relief; the snake-like tangles of a noctuid loosened, relaxed; a smooth viper seemed to slide down along the length of his body, eagerly slipping to the ground. He saw nothing, for the moon had hidden itself behind a cloud. His head weighed terribly, his temples pounded loudly . . . .

Suddenly he jumped up from the bedding and feverishly

looked for some matches. He found them, tore them open, and lit a taper. A faint light brightened up the room; no one was there.

He leaned over the bed. The bedding was spread with soot, full of signs of the bodies that had rolled over it; on the pillow there were several large blood stains. Then he saw that his left hand was tightened about a knife spattered with gore up to the handle.

He was seized by a dull dizziness. Staggering, he rushed to the window and opened it; a freezing gust of winter morning air came in and hit him in the face. Out of the room escaped a trail of lethal gas . . . .

He regained consciousness, he remembered the cry. Automatically, half-clothed, he dashed with the lit taper toward the inner room. Standing at the threshold, he glanced inside, and bridled up.

On a filthy plank-bed lay two naked corpses – the gigantic old man's and Makryna's – steeped profusely in blood. Both had the same fatal wound, near the left armpit, above the heart . . . .

THE MOTION DEMON

The express *Continental* from Paris to Madrid rushed with all the force its pistons could muster. It was already the middle of the night; the weather was showery. The beating rain lashed the brightly lit windows and was scattered on the glass in rolling drops. Bathed in the downpour, the coaches glittered under roadside lampposts like wet armour. A hollow groan issued forth into space from their black bodies, a confused chatter of wheels, jostling buffers, mercilessly trampled rails. The frenzied chain of coaches awakened sleeping echoes in the quiet night, drew out dead voices in the forests, revived slumbering ponds. Some type of heavy, drowsy eyelids were raised, some large eyes opened in consternation, and so they remained in momentary fright. And the train sped on in a strong wind, in a dance of autumn leaves, pulling after it an extended swirling funnel of startled air, while smoke and soot lazily clung to its rear; the train rushed breathlessly on, hurling behind it the blood-red memory of sparks and coal refuse . . . .

In one of the first-class compartments, squeezed in the corner, dozed a man in his forties, of strong, Herculean build. The subdued lamplight that filtered with difficulty through the drawn shade lit up his long, carefully shaved face and revealed his firmly set, thin lips.

He was alone; no one interrupted his sleepy reveries. The quiet of the closed interior was disturbed only by the knocking of wheels under the floor or the flickering of gas in the gas-bracket. The red colour of the plush cushions imbued a stuffy, sultry tone which acted soporifically like a narcotic. The soft, yielding material muffled sounds, deadened the rattle of the rails, and surrendered in a submissive wave to any pressure. The compartment appeared to be plunged into deep sleep: the curtains drawn on ringlets lay dormant, the green net spread under the ceiling swung lethargically. Rocked by the car's steady motion, the traveller leaned his weary head on the headrest and slept. The book that had been in his hands slipped from his knees to the floor. On its binding of delicate, dark-saffron vellum the title was visible: *Crooked Lines*; near that, impressed with a stamp, the name of the book's owner: Tadeusz Szygon.

At some moment the sleeper stirred; he opened his eyes and swept them about his surroundings. For a second an expression of amazement was reflected on his face. It seemed as if he couldn't understand where he was and why he found himself there. But almost immediately a wry smile of resignation came to his lips. He raised his large, powerful hand in a gesture of surrender, and then an expression of dejection and contemptuous disdain passed over his face. He fell back into a half-sleepy state . . . .

Someone's steps were heard in the corridor; the door was pulled back and a conductor entered the compartment:

'Ticket, please.'

Szygon didn't stir. Assuming he was asleep, the conductor came up and grasped him by the shoulder:

'Pardon me, sir; ticket, please.'

With a faraway look in his eyes, Szygon glanced at the intruder:

'Ticket?' he yawned out casually. 'I don't have one yet.'

'Why didn't you buy it at the station?'

'I don't know.'

'You're going to have to pay a fine.'

'F–fine? Yes,' he added, 'I'll pay it.'

'Where did you get on? Paris?'

'I don't know.'

The conductor became indignant.

'What do you mean you don't know? You're making fun of me, sir. Who else should know?'

'It doesn't matter. Let's assume that I got on at Paris.'

'And to what destination should I make the ticket out for?'

'As far as possible.'

The conductor looked carefully at the passenger:

26

'I can only give you a ticket as far as Madrid; from there you can transfer to any train you like.'

'It doesn't matter,' replied Szygon, with a wave of his hand. 'As long as I just keep on riding.'

'I will have to give you your ticket later. I must first issue it and work out the cost with the fine.'

'As you wish.'

Szygon's attention suddenly became riveted by the railway insignias on the conductor's collar: several jagged little wings weaved in a circle. As the sardonically smiling conductor was preparing to leave, Szygon sensed that he had already seen that face, twisted in a similar grimace, a few times before. Some fury tore him from his place, and he threw out a warning:

'Mr. Wings, watch out for the draft!'

'Please be quiet; I'm closing the door.'

'Watch out for the draft,' he stubbornly repeated. 'One can sometimes break one's neck.'

The conductor was already in the corridor.

'He's either crazy or drunk,' he remarked under his breath, passing into the next car.

Szygon remained alone.

He was in one of his famous 'flight' phases. On any given day, this strange person found himself, quite unexpectedly, several hundred miles from his native Warsaw and somewhere at the other end of Europe – in Paris, in London, or in some third-rate little town in Italy. He would wake up, to his extreme surprise, in some unknown hotel which he looked at for the first time in his life. How he came to be in such strange surroundings, he was never able to explain. The hotel staff, when questioned, generally measured the tall gentleman with a curious, sometimes sarcastic glance and informed him about the obvious state of things – that he had arrived the day before on the evening or morning train, had eaten supper and had ordered a room. One time some wit asked him if he also needed to be reminded under what name he had arrived. The malicious question was completely legitimate: a person who could forget what had occurred the previous day could also forget his own name. In any event, there was in Tadeusz Szygon's improvised rides a certain mysterious and unexplained feature: their aimlessness, which entailed a strange amnesia toward everything that had occurred from the moment of departure to the moment of arrival at an unknown location. This emphatically attested to the phenomenon being, at the very least, puzzling.

After his return from these adventurous excursions, life would go on as usual. As before, he would frequent the casino, lose his money at bridge and make his famous bets at horse races. Everything went along as it always had — normal, routine and ordinary . . . .

Then, on a certain morning, Szygon would disappear once again, vanishing without a trace . . . .

The reason for these flights was never made clear. In the opinion of some, one had to look for its source in an atavistic element inherent in the nature of this eccentric; in Szygon's veins there apparently flowed gypsy blood. It seemed he had inherited from his perpetually roaming ancestors a craving for constant roving. One example given as proof of this 'nomadism' was the fact that Szygon could never reside long in any one place: he was continually changing his living quarters, moving from one section of town to the other.

Whatever impulses prompted his aimless romantic travels, he certainly didn't glorify in them after his return. He would come back — likewise unexpectedly — angry, exhausted and sullen. For the next few days he would lock himself in his home, clearly avoiding people, before whom he felt shame and embarrassment.

Most interesting of all was Szygon's state during these 'flights' — a state almost completely dominated by subconscious elements.

Some dark force tore him from his home, propelled him to the railway station, pushed him into a carriage — some overpowering command impelled him, frequently in the middle of night, to leave his cosy bed, leading him like a condemned man through the labyrinth of streets, removing from his way a thousand obstacles, to place him in a compartment and send him out into the world. Then came a blindfolded, random journey, changing trains without any destination in mind, and a stop at a foreign city, or an out-of-the-way town or village, not knowing why precisely there and not some other place – and finally a terrible awakening in completely unfamiliar surroundings . . . .

Szygon never arrived at the same place: the train always put him off at a different destination. During his ride he never 'woke up,' i.e., he never became aware of the aimlessness of what he was doing – his full psychic faculties returned only after his departure from the train, and this frequently only after a deep, fortifying sleep in a hotel or a roadside shed or inn . . . .

At the present moment he was in an almost trance-like state. The train now carrying him had departed yesterday morning from Paris. Whether he got on at the French capital or at some station along the route, he didn't know. He had departed from somewhere and was now heading somewhere else – that's all he could say . . . .

He adjusted himself on the cushions, stretched out his legs, and lit a cigar. He felt distaste, almost repugnance. He always experienced similar feelings at the sight of a conductor or, for that matter, any railwayman. These people were a symbol of certain deficiencies or of an underdevelopment, and personified the imperfection that he saw in the railway system. Szygon understood that he made his unusual journeys under the influence of cosmic and elemental forces, and that train travel was a childish compromise caused by the circumstances of his earthly environment. He realized only too well that if it weren't for the sad fact that he was chained to the Earth and its laws, his travels, casting off the usual pattern and method, would take on an exceedingly more active and beautiful form.

It was precisely the railway and its employees that embodied for him that rigid formula, that vicious circle from which he, a man, a poor son of the Earth, tried vainly to break out of.

That is why he despised these people; sometimes, he even hated them. This aversion to 'servants of a charter for leisurely rambling,' as he contemptuously called them, increased in direct proportion to his fantastic 'flights,' of which he was ashamed not so much for their aimlessness, but rather because they were conceived on such a pitiful scale.

This feeling of detestation was augmented by the little incidents and quarrels with the train authorities that were inevitable due to his unnatural state. On certain lines the employees seemed to already know him well, and during his journeys he would frequently detect the cruel smile of a porter, conductor or railway official.

The conductor attending the coach he was now riding seemed to be particularly familiar. That lean, pitted face – lit up with a jeering little smile at the sight of him – had passed before his dreamy, faraway eyes not just once. At least, that's what he thought . . . .

But most of all Szygon was irritated by railway advertisements and uniforms. How funny was the pathos of those travel allegories hanging about waiting rooms, how pretentious the sweeping gestures of those little geniuses of speed! Yet the most comical impression was created by those winged circles on the caps and lapels of the officials. What nerve! What fantasy! At the sight of these insignias, Szygon frequently had the urge to tear them off and replace them with a likeness of a dog chasing its own tail . . . .

His cigar glowed peacefully, filling the compartment with small clouds of bluish smoke. Little by little the fingers holding the cigar lazily loosened and the fragrant trabuco rolled under the seat, spattering a rocket of tiny sparks. Szygon was asleep . . . .

A fresh release of steam in the pipes lisped quietly under his feet, spreading a cosy warmth about the compartment. A mosquito, unusual for the season, hummed a faint song, made a few nervous circles and hid itself in a dark recess among plush protuberances. And once again there was only the gentle flicker of the gas-burner and the rhythmic clatter of wheels . . . .

At some time during the night Szygon woke up. He rubbed his forehead, changed his sleeping position, and glanced about the compartment. To his surprise and displeasure he noticed that he was not alone: he had a travelling companion. Opposite him, spread out comfortably on the cushions, sat a railway official puffing on a cigarette and impertinently exhaling the smoke in his direction. Beneath this person's neglectfully unbuttoned jacket Szygon could see a velvet vest, and he was reminded of certain station-master with whom he had had a blazing row. The railway official had, however, a familiar blood-red kerchief wrapped around his neck, just under a stiff collar with three stars and several winged circles, and this reminded Szygon of the insolent conductor who had irritated him earlier with his little smile.

'What the devil?!' he thought, carefully looking at the intruder's physiognomy. 'Why, quite clearly it's the loathsome face of that conductor! The same emaciated, sunken cheeks, the same smallpox marks. But from where did he get that rank and uniform?'

Meanwhile the 'intruder' apparently noticed the interest of his fellow traveller. He let out a cone of smoke and, after lightly brushing ash from his sleeve, put his hand to the peak of his cap and greeted him with a very sweet smile:

'Good evening!'

'Good evening,' Szygon answered dryly.

'Have you been travelling far?'

'At the moment I'm not in a social mood. I generally like to travel in silence. That's why I usually choose a solitary compartment and pay extra for the pleasure.'

Undeterred by the blunt retort, the railwayman smiled delightfully and continued with great composure:

'It doesn't matter. You'll slowly acquire the verve for speaking. It's just a question of practise and habit. Solitude

31

is, as is known, a bad companion. Man is a social animal – *zoon politikon* – isn't that true?'

'If you want to consider yourself an animal, I personally have nothing against it. I am just a man.'

'Excellent!' the official pronounced. 'See how your tongue has loosened. It's not as bad as it seems. On the contrary, you possess a great talent for conversation, particularly in the direction of parrying questions. We'll slowly improve. Yes, yes,' he added patronizingly, 'somehow we'll make a go of it; somehow.'

Szygon squinted his eyes and studied the intruder.

After a moment of silence, the persistent railwayman continued: 'Unless I'm mistaken we are old acquaintances. We've seen each other several times in the past.'

Szygon's resistance slowly melted. The insolence of this person who insulted him with impunity, and for no apparent reason, disarmed him. He became interested in knowing more about this 'station-master.'

'It's possible,' he said, after clearing his throat. 'Only it seems to me that until recently you wore some other uniform.'

At that moment a curious metamorphosis transformed the railwayman. The shirt with the glittering gold tinsel stars disappeared, the red railway cap vanished, and now, instead of the kindly-smiling station-master, sat opposite Szygon the stooping, dishevelled and sneering conductor, with his shabby jacket, and the ever-present bouquet of small lanterns attached to his person.

Shocked, Szygon rubbed his eyes:

'A transformation? Poof! Magic or what?!'

But already leaning toward him was the kindly 'station-master,' equipped with all the insignias of his office, while the conductor had hidden himself inside the uniform of a superior.

'Ah, yes,' he said casually, as if the process were nothing, 'I've been promoted.'

'I congratulate you,' muttered Szygon, staring with amazement at the quick-change artist.

'Yes, yes,' the other chatted, 'there "above" they know how to value energy and efficiency. They recognize a good person: I've become a station-master. The railway, my dear sir, is a great thing. It is worthwhile to spend one's life in its service. A civilizing element! A swift go-between of nations, an exchange of cultures! Speed, my dear sir, speed and motion!'

Szygon disdainfully pursed his lips.

'Mr. Station-master,' he underlined scoffingly, 'you're surely joking. What kind of motion? Under today's conditions, with improved technology, that excellent locomotive, the so-called "*Pacific Express*" in America, runs at 200 kilometres an hour; if we grant in due time a further increase to 250 kilometres, even 300 kilometres – what of it? We are looking at an end result; despite everything, we haven't gone out even a millimetre beyond the Earth's sphere.'

The station-master smiled, unconvinced. 'What more do you want, sir? A wonderful velocity! 200 kilometres an hour! Long live the railway!'

'Have you gone crazy?' asked Szygon, already furious.

'Not at all. I gave a cheer to the honour of our winged patron. How can you be against that?'

'Even if you were able to attain a record 400 kilometres – what is that in the face of absolute motion?'

'What?' said the intruder, pricking up his ears. 'I didn't quite get that – absolute motion?'

'What are all your journeys, even with the greatest speed imaginable, even on the farthest extended lines, in comparison to absolute motion and the fact that, in the end, despite everything, you remain on the ground. Even if you could invent a devilish train that would circumvent the entire globe in one hour, eventually you'd return to the same point you started from: you are chained to the ground.'

'Ha, ha!' scoffed the railwayman. 'You are certainly a poet, my dear sir. You can't be serious?'

'What kind of influence can even the most terrific,

fabulous speed of an earthly train have on absolute motion and its effect.'

'Ha, ha, ha!' bellowed the amused station-master.

'None!' shouted Szygon. 'It won't change its absolute path by even an inch; it won't change its cosmic route even by a millimetre. We are riding on a globe turning in space.'

'Like a fly on a rubber ball. Ha, ha, ha. What thoughts, what concepts! You are not only a first-class conversationalist, but a splendid humorist as well!'

'Your pathetic train, your ant-like, frail train with its best, boldest "speed," as you like to term it, relies – notice, I'm clearly underlining this – relies simultaneously on twenty relative motions, of which every one on its own is by far stronger and unquestionably more powerful than your miniature momentum.'

'Hmm ... interesting, most fascinating!' derided the unyielding opponent. 'Twenty relative motions – a substantial number.'

'I've omitted the incidental ones which for certain no railwayman has even dreamed of, and will mention the principal, pivotal ones known to every schoolboy. A train rushing with the greatest fury from A to B has to simultaneously make a complete rotation with the Earth round its axis in a twenty-four hour period . . . .'

'Ha, ha, ha! That's novel, absolutely novel . . . .'

'At the same time it whirls with the entire globe around the sun . . . .'

'Like a moth around a lamp . . . .'

'Spare me your jokes! They're not interesting. But that's not all. Together with the Earth and the Sun, the train goes along an elliptical line, relative to the constellation Centaurus, toward some unknown point in space to be found in the direction of the constellation Hercules.'

'Philology at the service of astronomy. *Parbleu*! How profound!'

'You're an idiot, my dear sir! Let's move over to the incidental motions. Have you ever heard anything about the Earth's precessional movement?'

'Maybe I've heard something about it. But what does all this concern us? Long live the motion of a train!'

Szygon fell into a rage. He raised his mallet-like hand and let it drop forcefully on the scoffer's head. But his arm cut only through air: the intruder had vanished somewhere; the space opposite was suddenly vacant.

'Ha, ha, ha!' chortled someone from the other corner of the compartment.

Szygon turned around and spotted the 'station-master' squatting between the headrest and the net; somehow he had contracted himself to a small size, and now looked like an imp.

'Ha, ha, ha! Well? Will we be civil in the future? If you want to talk further with me, then behave properly. Otherwise, I won't come down. A fist, my dear sir, is too ordinary an argument.'

'For thick-headed opponents it's the only one; nothing else can be as persuasive.'

'I've been listening,' the other drawled, returning to his old place, 'I've been listening patiently for quarter of an hour to your utopian theories. Now listen a little to me.'

'Utopian?!' growled Szygon. 'The motions I've mentioned are therefore fictitious?'

'I don't deny their existence. But of what concern are they to me? I'm only interested in the speed of my train. The only conclusive thing for me is the motion of engines. Why should I be concerned about how much forward I've moved in relation to interstellar space? One has to be practical; I am a positivist, my dear sir.'

'An argument worthy of a table leg. You must sleep well, Mr. Station-master?'

'Thank you, yes. I sleep like a baby.'

'Of course. That's easy to figure out. People like you are not tormented by the Motion Demon.'

'Ha, ha, ha! The Motion Demon! You'll fallen onto the gist of the matter! You've hit upon my profitable idea – actually, to tell the truth, not mine, but merely commissioned by me from a certain painter at our station.'

'A profitable idea? Commissioned?'

'Oh, yes. It concerns a just-issued prospectus for a couple of new railway branches – the so-called *Vergnügungsbahnlinien*. Consider this – a type of publicity or poster that would encourage the public to use these new lines of communication. And so some vignette, some picture was needed, something like an allegory, or a symbol.'

'Of motion?!' Szygon paled.

'Exactly. The aforementioned gentleman painted a mythical figure – a magnificent symbol that in no time swept through the waiting rooms of every station, not only in my country, but beyond its borders. And because I endeavoured to get a patent and stipulated a copyright in the beginning, I haven't done badly.'

Szygon raised himself from the cushions, straightening up to his full imposing height.

'And what figure did your symbol assume, if its possible to know?' he hissed in a choked, strange voice.

'Ha, ha, ha! The figure of a genius of motion. A huge, swarthy young man balanced on extended raven wings, surrounded by a swirling, frenzied dance of planets – a demon of interplanetary gales, interstellar moon blizzards, wonderful, maddeningly hurling comets, comets and more comets . . . .'

'You're lying!' Szygon roared, throwing himself toward the speaker. 'You're lying like a dog.'

The 'station-master' curled up, diminished in size, and vanished through the keyhole. Almost at the same moment the compartment door opened, and the disappearing intruder merged into the figure of the conductor, who was at the threshold. The conductor looked at the perturbed passenger with a mocking smile and began to hand him a ticket:

'Your ticket is ready; the price, including the fine, is 200 francs.'

But his smile was his ruin. Before he got a chance to figure out what was happening, some hand, strong like destiny, grabbed him by the chest and pulled him inside. A desperate cry for help was heard, then the cracking of bones. A dull silence followed.

After a moment, a large shadow moved along the windows of an empty corridor and toward the exit. Somebody opened the coach door and pulled the alarm signal. The train began to brake abruptly . . . .

The dark figure hurried down a couple of steps, leaned in the direction the train was moving, and with one leap jumped between roadside thickets glowing in the dawn light . . . .

The train halted. The uneasy crew searched for a long time for the person who pulled the alarm; it wasn't known from which coach the signal had come. Finally the conductors noticed the absence of one of their colleagues. 'Coach No. 532!' They rushed into the corridor and began to search through the cubicles. They found them empty, until in the last one, a first-class compartment at the end, they found the body of the unfortunate man. Some type of titanic force had twisted his head in such a hellish manner that his eyes had popped out of their sockets and were gazing at his own chest. In the plucked whites, the morning sun played a cruel smile . . . .

THE AREA

For more than twelve years Wrzesmian had not written a word. After publishing in 1900 the fourth in his series of original, insanely strange works, he became silent and irrevocably removed himself from the public eye. From that time on he didn't touch his pen, he didn't even express himself with a trivial verse. He wasn't wrested from silence by his friends' urgings, nor was he stirred by the attentive voices of critics who speculated about a forthcoming work of epic proportions. These anticipations passed, and nothing was heard from Wrzesmian.

Slowly an obvious conclusion, as bright and clear as the sun, began to form concerning him: he had exhausted himself prematurely. 'Yes, yes,' the heads of the literati sadly nodded, 'he wrote too much too soon. He didn't understand the economy of production; he touched on a few too many issues in one work. He actually offended with an overabundance of ideas, which, compressed into dense summaries, weighed down the forceful material. The potion was too strong; it deserved, rather, to be given in smaller, diluted doses. He damaged his own reputation: he ran out of things to say.'

These judgements reached Wrzesmian, but they did not elicit the slightest response. Consequently, his speedy impoverishment was believed in, and the world paid him no heed. Besides, new talents emerged, new figures appeared on the horizon. Finally he was left in peace.

And, indeed, the majority of people were glad with this turn of events. Wrzesmian wasn't too popular. The works of this strange man, saturated with rampant fantasy and imbued with strong individualism, gave a most unfavourable impression by inverting accepted aesthetic-literary theories and by mocking established pseudo-truths. His output was eventually acknowledged as the product of a sick imagination, the bizarre work of an eccentric, maybe even a madman. Wrzesmian was an inconvenience for a variety of reasons, and he disturbed unnecessarily, stirring peaceful waters. Thus his premature eclipse was received with a secret sigh of relief.

And no one supposed even for a moment that the cause of his withdrawal from the public eye was not the loss of his literary powers. Wrzesmian, however, was utterly indifferent as to what was, or would be, said about him. He considered the whole affair personal and private, and never thought of extricating himself from people's mistaken opinion.

And why should he? If what he wished for would realize itself, the future would reveal the truth and burst the hardened shell he had been sealed in; but if his dreams did not come true, he would be less than convincing and would expose himself only to ridicule. Thus it was better to wait and be silent.

For Wrzesmian was not lacking in breath and force but was instead seized with new desires. He wanted to attain better means of expression, and he began to aim for something creative that would prove far more significant and authentic. Already the written word was not enough for him: he was searching for something more direct, he was seeking greater artistic material to fulfil his ideas.

The situation was so tied up with this, and his dreams were so impractical, that the path of creation he was treading departed far from the beaten track.

Ultimately most works of art revolve, more or less, in a realistic sphere, reproducing or transforming the sights of life. Events, though fabricated, are only its analogy, intensified, admittedly, through exaltation or pathos, and therefore possible at some moment in time. Similar scenes might have once occurred in reality, they may be realized sometime in the future, nothing prevents a belief in their possibility – reason doesn't rebel against feasible artistic creations. Even most works of fantasy do not exclude probable realization, unless they show an inclination toward pranks or the heedless smirk of a skilful juggler.

But in Wrzesmian's case the matter presented itself a little differently. The whole of his strange, enigmatic work was one great fiction. In vain had the pack of critics, as cunning as foxes, laboured in search of so-called 'literary influences,' 'analogies,' 'foreign strains' that would, even if roughly, give a clue to the impenetrable castle of Wrzesmian's poetry; in vain had shrewd reviewers run for help to learned psychiatric experts, sifted through all manner of writings, immersed themselves in encyclopedias: the writings of Wrzesmian emerged triumphant over successful interpretation, even more mysterious, bewildering and dangerous than before. A gloomy spell exuded from them, an alluring, vertiginous, bone-chilling depth.

Despite their total fantasy, never once touching reality, Wrzesmian's writings jolted, puzzled and amazed: people never dared to venture past them with just a shrug of the shoulders. Something resided in these short and dense works that riveted the attention and fettered the soul; a powerful   suggestion   arose   from   these   incisive compendium-like works – written in such a seemingly cold style, as if a reporter's or a teacher's – under which pulsated the fervour of a fanatic.

For Wrzesmian had believed in what he had been writing; for he had acquired as time went on the firm conviction that any thought, even the most audacious, that any fiction, even the most insane, can one day materialize and see its fulfilment in space and time.

'No person thinks in vain; no thought, even the strangest, disappears fruitlessly,' he used to repeat many times to his circle of friends and acquaintances.

And it seemed that it was precisely this belief in the materialization of fiction that caused a hidden flame to flow through the arteries of his works, for despite their apparent coldness, they penetrated to the core . . . .

But he was never satisfied. Like every creative artist, he was constantly seeking new means of expression and ever more distinct symbols that would represent his thoughts in the best possible manner. Finally he had abandoned the written word, scorning language as a too crude form of expression, and began to yearn for something more direct that would artistically and tangibly outdistance all that had gone before. It was not silence he sought – the 'resting of the word' of the symbolists; that was for him too pale, too nebulous – and lacking in sincerity. He wanted something else.

What that something would be, he didn't precisely know, but he firmly believed in its possibility. A few facts garnered while he still wrote and published had strengthened this belief. He had convinced himself even then that despite the imaginary character of his creations, they possessed a particular energy that could flow out into the world. The crazy thoughts of Wrzesmian, coming out from the incandescent content of his work, seemed to have had a fertilizing-like power, and he saw their manifestations flare up unexpectedly in the acts and gestures of certain individuals, in the course of certain events.

But even this had not been enough. He desired creative realizations that would be completely independent of the laws of reality, realizations that would be as free as their source – fiction; and as free as their origin – dreams. This would be the ideal – the highest achievement, a complete, full expression without a shadow of insufficiency . . . .

Wrzesmian understood, however, that such an achievement might result in his own annihilation. Absolute fulfilment would also be a complete release of one's energy, causing death through a surfeit of artistic exertion. Because the ideal, as is known, is in death. A work overwhelms the author with its weight. Thoughts fully realized can become threatening and vengeful, especially thoughts that are insane. Left alone, without a point of support on a real base, they can be fatal to their creator.

Wrzesmian had a presentiment of this eventuality, but he wasn't swayed, nor frightened. His desire dominated everything else . . . .

Meanwhile the years went silently by without eliciting the materializations he longed for. Wrzesmian completely estranged himself from the world, taking up solitary residence at the outskirts of the city in a street that looked onto open fields. Here, enclosed in his two small rooms, cut off from society, he spent months and years in reading and contemplation. He slowly restricted himself to ever diminishing contact with daily life, to which he paid only minimal, unavoidable tribute. Besides, he was totally absorbed in himself, in his dreams and in longing for their fulfilment. His ideas, not projected on paper as before, took on strength and vitality; they grew through non-expression of their contents. Sometimes it seemed to him that his thoughts were not abstractions but something rich and substantial, that he could just about reach out and grasp them. But the illusion quickly blew away, leaving in its place only bitter disappointment.

Yet he didn't lose heart. In order not to be too distracted by the sights of the outside world, he limited the scope of his perceptions, which constantly seen without change, day after day, gradually entered through the years into the well-knit circle of his ideas and became commensurate with their terrain. Eventually these perceptions merged with the world of his dreams into one particular area.

Thus, imperceptibly, some unreachable habitat was formed, some secret oasis to which no one had access except Wrzesmian, king of this unseen world. This milieu, imbued with the ego of the dreamer, appeared to the uninitiated as a simple place in space; people could only perceive its exterior, physical existence – but the internal pulsations of fermenting thoughts, the subtle connection these had with Wrzesmian's own person, they failed to sense . . . .

By odd chance the place enveloped by the mind of the dreamer, and the one he transformed into the area of his dreams, was not his home. The oasis of his fiction arose opposite his windows, on the other side of his street, in the form of a two-storied villa.

The gloomy elegance of the house captivated him from the first moment he had occupied his new abode. At the end of a black double row of cypresses, their two lines containing a stone pathway, appeared a several-stepped terrace where a weighty, stylized double door led to the interior. Across the iron railing that surrounded the mansion, the wings of the house were losing colour. Sickly and sad walls, coated with a pale-greenish paint, peered out from inside. From underneath the garden, treacherously concealed humidity crawled out here and there with dark oozing. Once carefully cultivated flowers had with time lost the orderliness of their arrangement. Only two eternal fountains quietly wept, shedding water from marble basins onto clusters of rich, red roses. Only a muscular Triton on the left side continually raised his hand in the same gesture of greeting to a limber Harpy who, leaning from a marble cistern on the other side, enticed him for many years with the lure of a divine body; in vain, because they were separated by the mournful cypresses . . . .

The celadon villa gave the impression of dismal loneliness, abandoned by its inhabitants a long time ago and isolated from neighbouring buildings. It ended the street; there were no other houses beyond it – only wide bands of marshy meadows, fallows, and, in the distance, beech woods that turned black during winter and a rust-colour during autumn . . . .

No one had been living in the villa for a number of years. The owner, a wealthy aristocrat, had long since gone abroad, leaving the house without a caretaker.

Thus it stood neglected in the middle of the overgrown garden, wasted away by corrosive rain and crumbling under the malice of winds and winter blizzards.

The dreary spell that blew from this retreat stirred Wrzesmian's soul. The villa was for him an architectural embodiment of the mood which pervaded his work; gazing intently on it, he felt as if he were in his own home.

That is why he spent entire hours by his window, resting on the frame and casting his musing eyes in the direction of that sad house. He especially liked to observe on lunar nights the effects evoked on the fantastic retreat by the moon's light. Night-time, in fact, seemed to be its real element. During the day the villa was dormant as if in lifeless sleep. The magic hidden in its mysterious interior appeared in its entirety only after the setting of the sun. Then the house came back to life. Some intangible tremor coursed through the sleeping hermitage, shook the cypresses solidified in mourning, rippled weathered pediments and friezes . . . .

Wrzesmian watched and lived the life of the house. Precise thoughts were awakened within him, harmonious with the scenery across the street; pathetic tragedies were born, as strong as death, as menacing as fate; then again, some vague thoughts loomed, dimmed as if by the moon's silver patina.

Every recess became a sensory counterpart to a fiction, a material realization of thoughts that clung onto ledges, roamed about forlorn rooms, wept on terrace steps. Jumbled crazy dreams and hazy imaginings roved in fluid dispersion and wandered along walls, uncertain of support. But even these found a haven. Irritated by the capriciousness of their movement, the imagination thrust them away with contempt, so that, frightened, they flowed down in filmy streams into a large moss-grown vat at the corner of the house, moving into its black body somnolently, torpidly, like rain on autumn days. Faint, rusty thoughts, slightly acidic . . . .

Wrzesmian got drunk with the gloomy frolics of these fantasies, letting their creations run loose. According to his whim he changed their direction or drove them away from sight, in the next moment conjuring up replacements . . . .

No one bothered him. The secluded street in the distant quarter of the city was not disturbed by any inopportune intruder; no noisy cart interrupted the atmosphere.

Thus he had spent the last several years – years untouched by the outside, but full of menace and marvels from within.

Until suddenly one day some changes occurred in the

44

house across the street, instantly stopping the fantasies that had already started to adopt forms set by habit and practice.

It happened one fine July evening. Sitting, as usual, by an open window, his head propped up by his hand, Wrzesmian had been sweeping a meditative glance about the villa and the garden. All of a sudden, looking into one of the windows in a wing of the house, he shuddered. By the windowpane, gazing stubbornly at him, was the pale face of a man. The unmoving gaze of the strange stare was sinister. Wrzesmian became seized with a vague dread. He rubbed his eyes, walked about his room a couple of times, and looked again at the window: the severe face had not disappeared, but continued to stare in his direction.

'Has the owner of the villa returned?' Wrzesmian threw out the feeble supposition in an undertone.

In answer, a sarcastic smile twisted the features of the dreary mask. Wrzesmian pulled down the blind and lit up his home: he couldn't endure the gaze any longer.

To obliterate these impressions he immersed himself in reading until midnight. At twelve he wearily raised himself from a book, and drawn by an overpowering temptation, he lifted the edge of the blind to peek out of the window. And again a shudder of fear chilled him to the bone: the pale man was still there, standing motionless by the window in the right wing. Illuminated by the bright magnesium shine of the moon, he paralyzed Wrzesmian with his gaze. Uneasy, Wrzesmian returned the blind to its position and tried to fall asleep. In vain. His imagination, imbued with dread, tormented him terribly. It was already morning before he finally fell into a short, nervous sleep, and even then it was one full of nightmares and visions. When he woke up around noon, with a giddy head, his first thought was to look at the villa's windows. He breathed a sigh of relief: the obstinate face was gone.

Throughout the day there was peace. But at evening he saw, by a window on the first floor, the mask of a woman staring at him, her streaming hair bordering a face already

45

withered but with traces of her former beauty, a face maddened by a pair of wild, intense eyes. And she was looking at him through frenzied pupils with the same severe gaze as her companion from the right wing. Both seemed unaware of their coexistence in the strange house. They were joined only by their menacing gesture directed toward Wrzesmian . . . .

And again after a sleepless night, interrupted by looking at his persecutors, a day free of masks followed. But as soon as dusk was entering into its secret conspiracy with the night, a third new figure appeared by another window and it also did not retreat until dawn. In the space of several days all the windows of the villa were filled up with sinister faces. From behind every window looked out a pair of despairing eyes, or ovals marked with suffering and madness. The house gazed at him with the eyes of maniacs, the grimace of lunatics; it grinned toward him with the smile of the demented. Not one of these people had he seen in his life, and yet all of them were somehow known to him. But he knew not from where. Each one of them had a different expression, but all were united in their threatening demeanour; apparently he was considered a common enemy. Their hatred was terrifying, yet mesmerizing. And, strangely enough, in the deepest layers of his mind, he understood their anger and acknowledged its justness.

And they, as if fathoming him from afar, gathered certainty of expression, and their masks became more severe with every day.

Then one August night, while he was leaning out of his window, enduring the crucifying gazes of their hateful eyes, the immobile faces suddenly became animated; in each flashed simultaneously the same will. Hundreds of pale, thin hands raised themselves in a movement of command, and scores of bony fingers made beckoning motions . . . .

Wrzesmian understood: he was being summoned inside. As if hypnotized he leaped over the windowsill, crossed the

46

narrow street, jumped over the railing, and began to walk along the alley to the villa . . . .

It was four in the morning, the hour before dawn's tremblings. The magnesium jets of the moon bathed the house in a silver whirlpool, luring long shadows from its curves. The path was a dazzling white in the midst of sorrowful shrub walls. The hollow echo of Wrzesmian's steps reverberated on the stone slabs, as the fountains rippled quietly and their bent waters drizzled with unsolved mystery . . . . He went up the terrace and jerked strongly on the door handle: the door gave way. He walked along a lengthy corridor of two rows of Corinthian columns. The darkness brightened the glory of the moon, whose beams, pouring through a stained-glass panel at the end of the gallery, unreeled green fables onto porphyritic floor tiles . . . .

Suddenly, as he was walking, a figure emerged from behind the shaft of a column and followed him. Wrzesmian shuddered but silently went on. A couple of steps further a new figure detached itself from a niche between two columns; then a third, and a fourth . . . a tenth—all followed him. He wanted to turn back, but they blocked his way. He crossed the forest of columns and swerved to the right, into some circular hall. It was illuminated by the shimmering moon and crowded with strange people. He slipped between them, looking for an exit. In vain! They surrounded him in an increasingly closed circle. From pale, bloodless lips flowed out a menacing whisper:

'It's him! It's him!'

He stopped and looked defiantly at the throng:

'What do you want from me?'

'Your blood! We want your blood! Blood! Blood!'

'What do you want it for?'

'We want to live! We want to live! Why did you call us out from the chaos of non-existence and condemn us to be miserable half-corporeal vagrants? Look at how weak and pale we are!'

'Mercy!' he wailed, desperately throwing himself toward a winding staircase in the depth of the hall.

'Hold him! Surround him! Surround him!'

With the speed of a madman he ascended the stairs to the upper floor and burst into a medieval chamber. But his oppressors entered after him. Their slender arms, their fluid, damp hands joined in a macabre line.

'What did I do to you?'

'We want full life! You confined us to this house, you wretch! We want to go out into the world; we want to be released from this place to live in freedom! Your blood will fortify us, your blood will give us strength! Strangle him! Strangle him!'

Thousands of hungry mouths extended toward him, thousands of pale, sucking lips.

In a crazy reflex he flung himself toward the window, ready to jump out. A legion of slimy, cold hands seized him by the waist, dug crooked hook-like fingers into his hair, wrung his neck. He struggled desperately. Someone's fingernails cut into his larynx, someone's lips fastened to his temple . . . .

He staggered, supported himself on the embrasure with his shoulders, and leaned back. His convulsively extended arms spread out in a sacrificial movement; a weary smile of fulfilment crept over his whitened lips – he was already dead . . . .

At the moment when the interior cooled with the agonized throes of Wrzesmian's body, the pre-dawn silence was interrupted by a dull ripple. It came from the vat at the corner of the house. The surface of the water, mouldy from the green scum, seethed; inside the rotten barrel, encompassed by rusty hoops, swirls rose, refuse undulated, sediment gurgled. A couple of large, distended bubbles escaped, and a misshapen stump of a hand appeared. Some sort of torso or framework emerged from the depth, dripping with water, covered with mould and a cadaverous putridity – maybe a man, beast or plant. This monstrosity glinted its amazed face toward the sky, opened spongy lips wide in a vague imbecilic-enigmatic smile, extracted from the vat legs twisted as a thicket of coral, and, shaking the water off, started to walk with an unsteady, swinging step . . . .

Daybreak had already arrived; violet luminosities slithered about the boundless regions of the world.

The monstrosity was heading toward the deep-blue forest on the distant horizon. It opened the gate in the garden, hobbled on bowlegs along a narrow path, and, drenched in the amethystine streams of morning twilight, tottered toward fields and meadows slumbering in daybreak's obscurity. Slowly, the freakish figure diminished, became diluted, and started to expire . . . until it dissolved, dispersing in the gleams of early dawn . . . .

A TALE OF THE GRAVEDIGGER

For two years after the mysterious disappearance of Giovanni Tossati, gravedigger of the main cemetery in Foscara, the town's inhabitants, particularly those settled near the place of eternal rest, complained of continual disturbance by the souls of the dead. Apparently, one group was tormented by all sorts of nightmares, another group had the onset of sleep blocked by phantoms, while others were bothered during the evening by ghosts moving about noisily from room to room. Masses conducted in these houses and exorcisms carried out by the bishop over the graves didn't help. On the contrary, the unrest flowing from the main cemetery seemed to spread, almost infectiously, to other cemeteries, and soon the entire city fell victim to the capricious deceased.

Only the arrival of the learned archaeologist and art scholar, Master Vincent Gryf of Prague, and the effective advice he gave the distressed councillors of the town, put a stop to this dangerous phenomenon.

The master, carefully examining the main cemetery, and particularly its monuments and tombstones, released shortly afterwards a small volume entitled *Satanae opus turpissimum, seu coemeterii Foscarae, regiae urbis profana violatio.* This little book, a curiosity of its type, printed in the year 1500 in medieval Latin, today belongs to those rare works forgotten under piles of library dust.

On the basis of his scrupulous study of the tombs, Gryf came to the conclusion that the main cemetery at Foscara had succumbed to a desecration unprecedented in Christian history.

Vincent's claim was met at first with violent opposition and disbelief, as his reasoning was based on details too subtle for the unskilled eye of the community. But when artists and sculptors from neighbouring towns verified his judgement, then there was nothing left for the city councillors to do but gracefully accept the verdict and apply his advice.

And, in truth, Gryf's opinion was most interesting and unique. For he noticed the desecration precisely in those splendid monuments and eloquent inscriptions of which the Foscara cemetery was celebrated throughout the entire country, and which every traveller visiting charming Tuscany had to see at least once.

And yet, after his thorough examination, which lasted more than a month, Master Vincent showed that behind the pious, seemingly dignified works of art was hidden a sacrilege exhibiting truly devilish skill. The monuments, the marble sarcophagi and family tombs were one uninterrupted chain of blasphemies and satanic concepts.

From behind the hieratical poses of tomb angels appeared the vulgar gesture of a demon, on lips bevelled with suffering flickered an illusive smile of cynicism. Statues of women, bending with the agony of despair, aroused the libido with sumptuous bodies, unfurled hair, hypocritically bare breasts. The larger compositions, formed of several figures, created the impression of a double meaning, as if the sculptor had intentionally chosen *risqué* themes, for the boundary between lofty suffering and lewdness was ambiguous.

The least amount of doubt, however, was awakened by the inscriptions – those celebrated Foscara stanzas whose solemn cadences were admired by all lovers of poetry. These verses, when read backwards from bottom to top, were a scandalous, completely cynical denial of what was proclaimed in the opposite direction. They were rank paeans of honour for Satan and his obscene affairs, hymns of blasphemy against God and the saints, immoral songs of falernian wine and street harlots.

Such, in reality, was supposed to have been the cemetery. No wonder that the dead didn't want to lie there, that they raised an ominous revolt, demanding of the living the removal of the sacrilegious monuments.

Because of Gryf's findings, it was decided that the cemetery had to undergo a radical change. In the course of a few weeks all the suspect monuments and statues were shattered, the tombstones dug up and broken, and labourers carried off the pieces beyond the city. In their place, wealthy families put up new statues, while the poor stuck simple crosses on their family graves. The parish priest conducted obsequies in the cemetery chapel for three nights, ending with a great purification service.

And so, after the execution of all these acts, the dead stopped haunting the city, and the cemetery became soothed, plunging into the quiet reverie of previous years.

Then various stories began to circulate about what had happened, and slowly a legend developed in connection with the gravedigger, Giovanni Tossati, now nicknamed John Hyena.

Contributing considerably to these stories was the death of one of the gravedigger's helpers soon after the reconstruction of the cemetery. This person made a most interesting statement on his deathbed, which suddenly clarified Tossati's disappearance and spared the authorities a fruitless search for the supposedly fugitive criminal.

This confession, travelling from mouth to mouth, was spread widely about the region and, coloured with the exuberant imagination of the populace, with time entered into the circle of those gloomy tales which, stemming from nowhere, unreel their black thread on the spinning wheel of All Souls' Day evenings and frighten the children.

Giovanni Tossati had turned up at Foscara approximately twenty years earlier. Shabbily dressed, almost in rags, he immediately provoked suspicion, and the council even wanted to expel him from the city. Soon, though, he managed to gain the confidence of the inhabitants and the authorities, to whom he presented himself as an impoverished stonemason and sculptor of monuments. Given a trial examination, he demonstrated excellent skills and a seasoned hand in his craft. So, not only was he allowed to stay, but, owing to his oddly persistent pleas, he was appointed gravedigger of the main cemetery. From then on his job was to create monuments and bury the dead. He maintained that, for him, the simultaneous fulfilment of these two duties was an inseparable whole, that the rites for the dead were interwoven tightly with sepulchral art, and that he wouldn't be able to erect a monument to a deceased person if he couldn't bury him with his own hands. That's why later, even though his fame spread widely, he never accepted any of the more profitable positions offered from other regions; he immortalized the memory of the dead exclusively at his cemetery.

At first this eccentricity gave cause for jokes and derision, but in time people got used to the whims of the artist-gravedigger, as the works emerging from under his chisel soon earned praise from even the most knowledgeable of the *cognoscenti*. The previously modest cemetery became, in a dozen years or so, a sepulchral masterpiece and the pride of Foscara, which in turn became the envy of other cities.

From a ragged *lazzarone*, Tossati was transformed into a respected and wealthy citizen, a person of influence and prominence. Eventually he was elected chairman of the city council. Holding such a high office, he no longer personally dug graves, but now directed a large number of helpers, whom he taught in a truly novel manner. Tossati introduced into the burial trade a series of original improvements, cutting the work in half and quickening its tempo. He was no less faithful, though, to his old principles; he didn't neglect any burial and personally supervised the affair. After the corpse had been lowered into the grave, Tossati himself shovelled the first lump of earth onto the coffin, leaving the rest of the work to his labourers. In this manner his gravedigging functions took on, to a certain extent, a symbolic character, eliciting a pleasing memory of his former role; and not for all the money in the world would he abandon this particular custom.

Now, in general, Tossati was a strange person. His very appearance called attention to itself. Tall, broad-shouldered, his face wide and dreary, he was constantly smiling with a mysterious curl on his lips. His eyes were enigmatic, downcast. Maybe this downward gaze had adapted to his habit of bowing his head toward the ground, which he seemed to be carefully examining. The townspeople jokingly said that Tossati was sniffing for corpses.

Despite the renown of the gifted sculptor, the gravedigger was, in truth, not liked. People feared him and got out of his way. A superstition even developed that a meeting with him at an early hour of the day was a bad omen.

So, when after ten years in Foscara he decided to get married, none of the female inhabitants wanted to give him her hand. They were not tempted by Giovanni's vast prosperity, nor were they enticed by the promise of a life of affluence. In the end, he married a poor workwoman from a neighbouring village, an orphan given as a favour for an unfavourable fate.

But he didn't find happiness in family life. After a year of marriage his wife gave him twins: the first was stillborn; the second had been strangely formed in its mother's womb. This freak, dissimilar to any human baby, died on the third day after its birth. The broken-hearted woman disappeared one day, and all searches for her were in vain.

From then on he lived alone next to the cemetery in his white brick-walled house, and saw the townspeople mostly at funerals. Yet his windows were lit up late into the night, and neighbours frequently heard drunken shouts of people emanating from his home.

Nearly every night Tossati had some guests; but they were certainly not inhabitants of Foscara – at least no one in the city boasted of going there. Carriages drove up in front of the gravedigger's house, sometimes lavish coaches; strange people from unknown places would get out and go inside. At other times, heavy, usually empty wagons rolled in, creaking through the entrance gate, on which were loaded boxes and heavily boarded-up crates, to be taken away to an unknown destination before daybreak.

The city followed the sculptor's secretive movements

from a distance, not wanting to become involved in the affairs of a strange person who instilled fear in them.

By then the gravedigger and his home were enveloped in gloomy legends that had grown with the years and cemetery tales filled with rotting corpses and the stench of decay. It was said that the dead were visiting John and carrying on secret talks with him through the night. That's why no one was courageous enough to steal up to his brightly-lit windows and observe his guests.

Tossati knew of the tales surrounding him and didn't attempt to contradict them; on the contrary, it seemed as if he wanted to cocoon himself in ever thicker strands of mystery behind which he could hide his dark life.

The blasphemer's entire fortune arose from the cemetery; his home, possessions and life absorbed with time a corpse-like fustiness. And everything went along unpunished. As long as he walked the streets of Foscara, the dead seemed to patiently endure the affront. It was as if the evil demon residing in this person kept the world of shadows chained, as if the gravedigger's satanic will tethered any sign of revolt on the part of the desecrated deceased.

Tossati still walked around a little stooped and still smiled to no one in particular. In his last years of earthly tramping this smile never left his face, and it even seemed to have become gentle. During this time, Tossati's face gave the impression of a mummy with a set expression: it was the constantly smiling face of a good-natured soul.

For the stonemason had been wearing the same gypsum mask for two years. The material from which he had made it imitated so perfectly the colour of flesh, and the mask adhered so hermetically to his face, that it wasn't noticed at all: he went among people freely, not awakening either suspicion or laughter. Only an accident revealed his real face, a strange, unusual occurrence, after which one didn't see him any more among the living . . . .

It happened in autumn, on one of those sad, rainy days when the damp earth is enveloped by mists and plunges into gloomy pensiveness. In the afternoon, amidst threatening grey skies, a funeral took place. The town was burying its richest inhabitant, a widely esteemed merchant and owner of the silk mill. The great funeral procession – comprised of the town's first families, the representatives of every trade and the flower of the city's youth – accompanied the deceased to the cemetery, where he was placed in his family tomb.

Tossati was in an excellent mood that day and furtively rubbed his hands with glee. The deceased was unusually rich and was laid in the tomb in very costly attire. As he was taking the body off the bier, the gravedigger noticed two diamond signets on the merchant's middle and little fingers and a priceless ruby stud on his chest. Furthermore, he hadn't buried anyone for a long while in such a good state of preservation and so well suited to anatomical explorations – the old professor from Padua would be most pleased. The double reward portended well; it necessitated, in truth, hard and laborious work, particularly as the tomb would be securely closed. Yet the affair would be worth the trouble.

Later that day, he got the sudden impulse to drop by The Hyena, an inn not far from the cemetery. This tavern, constructed years ago thanks to his covert efforts and funds, was given this odd name by an unknown carpenter who had arrived at the gravedigger's special request. The name was justified by the front of the building, which had a stone hyena arching its spotted back over the inn. Soon the inn became the meeting place of pall bearers and gravediggers, who after every burial carried on a wake of their own, drinking away their earnings.

Out of principle Giovanni didn't show himself in this den of gambling and drinking, though he liked to pass by in the evening and listen to the drunken gaiety of his people.

Despite this, he wasn't able to resist temptation that day and decided to spend some time there in disguise. He first put on the attire of a high-ranking noble; then he attached his inseparable mask, secured a beard over it, and further hid himself with a wide hat. Thus dressed, he entered the inn early to observe at his leisure the funeral celebrations of his 'children.'

That evening a considerable number of people, of various occupations and positions, were congregating at the inn — the season was raw, boredom stifled one at home, and a Saint's Day feast, which would start the next day, brought many customers from surrounding areas. The proprietor of the inn, a sly, roguishly smiling old man, ran from table to table like a spinning top; he curled himself up, hemmed and hawed, poured wine and encouraged the singing. A group of wandering gypsies, squatting in the corner of the room, played melancholic-wild songs.

Around nine o'clock Tossati's men entered, and the inn took on its true character.

Tossati didn't take part in the conversations. Squeezed in a dark corner of the room, he covered his face with the wide brim of his hat so that he wouldn't be recognized, and just consumed innumerable mugs of the honey wine in silence. He listened and observed.

People's humour was exceptional, the mood, particularly after the entrance of the cemetery workers, gay. Anecdotes abounded, witticisms sparkled, jokes exploded. Peter Randone, a tall, stick-like scoundrel, especially outdid his companions by describing lewd scenes from his own experiences.

After midnight the inn started to slowly empty. The customers, wearied from drinking, went out one by one from the smoke-filled room and disappeared into the black night. Tossati, having overdone it, fell asleep. His hand dropped lazily on the table, pulling off the hat from his leaden head. At some moment his body, overpowered by drink, slid from the bench and fell heavily to the floor. The gravedigger didn't wake up; intoxicated sleep overpowered him completely. The good-natured mask, hitching against the table leg, slipped off his face and rolled under the chair with a soft rustle. None of this was noticed in the general tumult, and Giovanni slept in peaceful delight under the bench, undisturbed by anyone. But when the inn emptied around two and only the black brotherhood of death remained, the well-dressed customer lying under the bench attracted the curious glances of the last revellers.

'That rascal really got drunk! Let's take a look at him in the light!'

'We'll see whose mama's boy it is!'

'Some rich merchant or cavaliere – a man about town in pursuit of adventure. Come on, let's get him out from under that bench!'

Several eager hands stretched out toward the sleeper and laid him on his back. But when they saw the face of the drunken man, everyone recoiled simultaneously. The cemetery men's eyes were lit up in horrified amazement. Because the body of the stranger, attired in elegant, soft garments, had a corpse's head. The deeply sunken eyes stared out with what seemed cold death; the yellow, shrivelled skin merged with the tint of the jutting cheek bones; the hairless, earless skull shone with the smoothness of glazed tibias . . . .

A vague murmur ran through the group. The affair made them uneasy. The first one to 'get his wits about him' was Randone:

'What kind of stupid joke is this! Which one of you dug out this corpse for this masquerade? Well, speak up while you still have the chance!'

Silence. They glanced at each other in astonishment, not understanding what this was all about. No one pleaded guilty.

'Ha!' resumed Randone, 'we'll let it go for the time being; we'll deal with the joker later on. Now let's take this body on our shoulders while there is still time and head straight for the cemetery! In two hours it'll be daybreak – we have to hurry before it gets light. If the town hears of this, we're done for!'

Silently they carried out the order. Six men raised Tossati and, placing him on their shoulders, made their way out toward the cemetery. They went quickly, glancing about in apprehension in case someone was watching. They didn't pay attention to the mud spattering them up to their knees as they sloshed through puddles of rainwater. A strange fear and their leader's command drove them on – or someone else's command, or an internal necessity. They didn't speak; they didn't feel the unusual temperature of the body; they didn't notice that the hands of the corpse still hadn't rotted; they didn't for a moment pay attention to the difference between the state of the head and the rest of the body. Just as long as they moved forward, as quickly as possible, so as to be finished with the whole affair!

They plunged into the cool paths of the cemetery; they passed the main road, crossed several side ones, and turned right, amongst the fresh graves. Here, beside a jasmine tree hidden by thickets, they stopped and lowered Tossati to the ground.

'To your shovels,' resounded the quiet order of Peter Randone.

They briskly grabbed the handles and began to scoop out wet lumps of earth.

In fifteen minutes the grave was already deep.

Randone spoke again. 'To the bottom with him!!'

Tossati didn't budge, he didn't stir; he slept soundly.

Eager black hands hurled him into the hole. The thud of the dropped body merged with the impact of shovels throwing back the earth. The men worked with rare fervour, as if in a mad race. In several minutes the hole was filled up. Freshly carried and hastily packed-down earth topped off the grave.

Then the group breathed freely. With soiled hands, they wiped pearly drops of sweat from their foreheads; they looked about with a strange, quizzical glance. Then, not saying anything, they took their shovels and put as much distance as possible between themselves and the grave . . . .

It was perhaps four in the morning. A light rain started to fall again, sifted as if through a sieve. Beaded tears flowed down from cemetery birches and ran silently along paths; damp and pendulant willows swung sadly in the wind. Dawn's grey radiance, passing through the wall of trees, studied with amazement the melancholy retreat. Some evil birds, blinded by the pall of night, flapped their wings ominously amongst the branches and dug themselves deeper into the leaves. The rain drizzled, the wind soughed in the trees, the dawn became misty . . . .

A long, black procession of Tossati's men moved out stealthily from the cemetery gate, their step heavy, uncertain, their heads bowed low . . . .

SZAMOTA'S MISTRESS

(Pages from a discovered diary)

And the rib, which the Lord God had taken from
man, made he a woman, and brought her unto the
man. And Adam said, This is now bone of my bones,
and flesh of my flesh: she shall be called Woman,
because she was taken out of Man. Therefore shall a
man leave his father and his mother, and shall cleave
unto his wife: and they shall be one flesh. *Genesis*
2:22–24

I have been intoxicated with joy for six days now and can
hardly believe my good fortune. Six days ago I entered a new
phase of life, one so markedly different than what preceded,
that it seems I am living through a great cataclysm.

I received a letter from her.

Since her departure abroad a year ago to an unknown
destination – this first wonderful sign from her I
cannot, I truly cannot believe it! I will faint from joy!

A letter from her to me! To me, someone completely
unknown to her, a humble, distant admirer with whom no
friendly relations had existed before, not even a fleeting
acquaintanceship. But the letter is genuine. I carry it continually with me, I do not part with it even for one second.
The name on the address is clear, without a doubt: Jerzy
Szamota. It is I, after all. Not believing my own eyes, I
showed the envelope to several acquaintances; everyone
looked at me with some amazement, then smiled and
confirmed that the address is legible and bears my name.

So she is returning home, returning in just a couple of
days, and the first person who will greet her at her door
will be I – I, whose adoring eyes barely dared to look up at
her during chance sightings on the street, on some park
lane, in the theatre, at a concert ....

If I could have to my credit at least one glance, or a brief smile from her proud lips — but no! She seemed to have been completely unaware of me. Until this letter, I had been certain she did not even know of my existence. Surely she hadn't noticed me all those years while I trailed after her like a distant, timid shadow? I was so discreet, so very unobtrusive! My yearning enveloped her with such a far-removed, delicate ray. Yet she must have sensed this. With a sensitive woman's instinct, she sensed my love and my meek, boundless adoration. It seems that the invisible bonds of attraction that existed between us all these years grew more powerful during our distant separation, and now they draw her to me.

My best wishes, my most beautiful one! At this evening hour, the day bows before me in bright, cheerful flashes, and with a raised head I hum a song in praise of your magnificence — my most wonderful Lady!

It is already Thursday. The day after tomorrow, at this time, I will see her. Not until then. Such is her expressed wish. I take her letter in my hand, that priceless lilac sheet from which escapes a subtle fragrance of heliotrope, and I read for the hundredth time:

Dear! Call at the house on 8 Green Street on Saturday, the 26th, at six in the evening. You will find the garden gate open. I will be waiting for you. Let the yearning of many years be fulfilled. Yours, Jadwiga Kalergis

The house on 8 Green Street! Her villa, The Lindens! A splendid, medieval-styled little mansion in the midst of a grand park, separated from the street by woods and a thick wire fence; the aim of nearly all my daily walks. How many times during the evening had I sneaked up to this quiet spot, searching with a racing heart for her shadow on the windowpanes! . . .

Impatient with waiting for the anticipated Saturday, I was already at her house several times attempting to gain entry; but I always found the garden gate closed – the handle yielded, but the lock did not spring open. She still had not returned. I should be patient and wait, but I am so unbearably excited. I do not eat, I cannot sleep; I only count the hours, the minutes. So much time remains! Forty-eight hours! ... Tomorrow I will spend the entire day on the river by her park. I will rent a boat and circle near her villa. Saturday I will spend the morning and part of the afternoon at the railway station. I have to welcome her, at least from afar. I know from her neighbours, who have not seen her for a year, that she has not yet returned. She has definitely postponed her arrival until the 26th of September – that is, on the day of my visit. In truth, I fear I won't come at an opportune time; after such a journey she will be extremely tired.

*   *   *

Saturday morning – that is, yesterday – I did not see her among the abundant crowds at the station. I waited until four in the afternoon for the second train, with the same result. Maybe she hadn't arrived? Or maybe she had come on the morning train and was already at home? In either case, I had to go to her villa and ascertain the truth.

Those two hours that separated us became an unbearable torment whose end I could hardly wait for. Entering a café, I drank a large amount of black coffee, smoked lots of cigarettes, and unable to sit still, I rushed back outside. Passing by a flower stall, I remembered the flowers I had ordered for today.

How absentminded of me! I would have completely forgotten!

I went and collected a bouquet of crimson roses and azaleas. The freshly-cut flowers, their fragrant buds emerging from a circle of ferns, shook gently in the evening breeze. The clocks of the city were approaching a quarter to six.

I wrapped the bouquet in paper and quickly left in the

direction of the river. In several minutes I was already on the other side of the bridge. With a nervous step I neared the villa. My heart beat wildly, my legs trembled. Finally I reached the gate and pressed down on the handle: it gave way. Dazed by happiness, I rested for several minutes against the park fence, unable to contain my emotions. So, she had returned!

My wandering gaze travelled along the rows of linden trees, which, arranged on opposite sides of the pathway, stretched in long lanes to the portal. Somewhere to the left, behind mulberry and dogwood shrubs, appeared the skeleton of an autumnal vine-covered arbor; red leaves drifted down a chaotic trellis containing already-withered ivies.

Flower-beds held the blossoms of autumn: chrysanthemums and asters. Yellow chestnut and brick-red maple leaves drizzled with quiet sadness on paths overgrown with grass and weeds. Dahlias bled under a dried-up marble cistern; large glass containers alternated rainbow colours . . . . In the midst of a privet, on a stone bench covered with a carpet of conifer needles, two finches twittered a song of flight. Deep within the alleys, in the darkening sunset light, spiders spun out their silky, silver threads . . . .

With both hands I pushed open the heavy front door, and after ascending some winding stairs, I found myself on the first floor. I was struck by the absence of life. The mansion looked deserted; no one met me, nowhere was there a sign of servants or any members of the household. Scattered large electric lamps illuminated, with their blindingly bright beams, empty halls and galleries.

In the antechamber, opened hospitably for my arrival, unoccupied coat-racks presented a lonely sight. Their smooth metallic knobs glittered with the cold reflection of polished copper. I removed my coat. At that moment the sound of the city's clocks flowed in through a large, open Gothic window: they tolled the sixth hour . . . .

I knocked on the door in front of me. There was no response from within. I became anxious. What should I do? Enter without permission? Maybe, fatigued by travel, she was fast asleep?

Suddenly the door opened, and she stood on the threshold. Her piercing, proud yet sweet eyes gazed at me from under the regal diadem of her chestnut hair. Her classical head, worthy of Poliklet's chisel, was crowned by an emerald-inlaid tiara. A soft, snow-white peplos, flowing in harmonious waves to sixteenth-century footwear, enveloped her statuesque figure. *Juno stolata*!

I bowed before her majesty. And she, withdrawing inside, let me pass with a gesture of her hand into a palatial apartment. It was a magnificent bedroom decorated exquisitely in the fashions of former times.

In silence, she sat inside a deep niche on a *giallo antico* bed.

I knelt on the carpet by her feet, laying my head on her knees. She embraced it in a warm, maternal movement and started to tenderly comb my hair with her fingers. We gazed endlessly into each other's eyes, unable to sate ourselves with what we saw. We were silent. Thus far not one word had fallen between us – as if we feared scaring away with a reckless sound the angel of bewitchment that fettered and united our souls.

Suddenly she leaned over and kissed me on the lips. Blood pounded in my head, the world turned round drunkenly – and my passion unleashed itself. I grabbed her roughly and, not sensing any resistance, threw her on the bed. With a quick, elusive movement, she unclasped the amber fibula on her shoulder, exposing before me her divine body. So I possessed her in boundless suffering and longing, my senses intoxicated and my heart enraptured, my soul frenzied and my blood burning.

Hours passed with the speed of lightning, short as its flashes and potent with happiness; racing moments flew by like the winds of the steppe – moments precious like rare pearls. Wearied by pleasure, we drifted off to exquisite dreams that were like the groves of paradise, like magical fairy-tales – only to awaken to day-dreams even more wonderful, more beautiful . . . .

When I finally opened my heavy eyelids near six in the morning and glanced around, fully conscious, Jadwiga was no longer at my side.

I dressed quickly. After waiting for her in vain for an entire hour, I returned home . . . .

I feel giddy, there's fire in my veins. I must have a fever because my lips are swollen and there's a strange bitter taste in my mouth. Walking about, I stagger and stumble against the furniture . . . .

I look at the world as if through a mist or a delightful veil of entrancement . . . .

*　　　　*　　　　*

The following day, after my return from the newspaper office, I found a letter from Jadwiga on my desk, in which she designated our next meeting. It was to take place at her villa and again on a Saturday evening. That date seemed too distant for me: I went to The Lindens on Tuesday afternoon. But the gate was closed. Irritated, I walked around the little mansion a few times in the hope of spotting her in one of the park alleys. But the paths were empty – the autumn wind alone was there, raising batches of withered leaves and mercilessly driving them into lengthy, sad rows. Even though it soon became completely dark, I did not glimpse any lights through the windows. The house was silent and dead, as if there were no one living in it. So it seems she spends her evenings in one of the rooms with a northern exposure – that is, on the side least accessible to a passerby's eye. Discouraged, I left.

Similar attempts on the following days met with the same result, and so I had to submit to her wish and wait until Saturday. Nevertheless it surprised me that during that entire week I did not see her, even once, in town, not at the theatre, nor on the tram. Apparently a dramatic change has occurred in her life-style. Jadwiga Kalergis, once the daily object of admiration by the city's dandies and Don Juans, the queen of parties, concerts and social events, now lives like a nun.

In truth, I am happy and proud because of this. I do not possess the vain ambition of those who like to irritate others with a glimpse of their own happiness. I do not desire to flaunt her before the world. On the contrary — this secrecy, this furtive element in our relationship, has an inexpressible charm. *Odi profanum vulgus* . . . .

*   *   *

Finally Saturday arrived. Throughout the morning I paced about aimlessly. My friends at the office laughed at me, maintaining that most surely I was in love.

'That Szamota is really crazy,' muttered the theatre reporter. 'For some time he's been completely mad. One can't speak to him.'

'A skirt! *Cherchez la femme!*' explained a very old reporter. 'Nothing else. Believe me.'

Punctually at six in the evening I entered her bedroom through the half-open door. Jadwiga was not yet present. On a splendidly laid-out table there was a cup of hot chocolate; a pyramid of pastries rose beside the cup, and a green liqueur glittered nearby.

I sat down facing the adjoining room and reached for a trabuco cigar from a chrysolite box. Suddenly my glance fell on a piece of paper placed between the cigars. I recognized her handwriting; it was meant for me.

Dear! Excuse my lateness. I went to town and will return in half-an-hour. Till then!

I kissed the note and concealed it near my bosom; then I drank the fragrant chocolate. After my first glass of liqueur, I felt somewhat drowsy. I lit up a new cigar, mechanically fixing my eyes on the wall opposite me, where a brilliant Greek shield, with Medusa at its centre, hung. The shield's shimmering chest had something strangely magnetic about it that arrested the eyes, fettered the will.

Soon my attention was completely focused on one bright

spot, on the snake-haired Gorgon's blazing eye. I couldn't draw myself away from this hypnotic centre. Gradually, I drifted into a peculiar state. My surroundings retreated to a never-ending distant background, to be replaced by gorgeously rich colours, an exotic fairyland, a tropical *fata morgana* . . . .

Suddenly I felt a pair of warm, soft arms about my neck and a sweet, lingering kiss on my lips. I roused myself from my absorption. Next to me stood Jadwiga, smiling seductively. I took her by the waist, pressing her to my chest.

'Forgive me,' I explained, 'I didn't hear you come in. That shield holds one's attention most strangely.'

She responded with a silent smile of indulgence.

Today she was even more beautiful. Her statuesque loveliness, framed in Greek attire, exuded marvellous enchantment. Under wonderful brows looked out proud black eyes, smouldering with the flame of desire. Oh, what a joy to move those marble breasts with a wave of passion, to chisel out of the face of a haughty Juno her cool serenity!

Leaning her against my arm, I cast a hungry look at her, sating for a long moment my thirsty eyes on the vastness of her beauty.

'Oh, how beautiful you are, my sweetheart, oh, how beautiful! But where are your tresses, your violet-scented tresses?' I demanded passionately, attempting to push away from her forehead the soft, immaculately white veil that covered her head tightly today. 'I want to stroke your hair, just like that first time – remember? I want to spread out that ambrosial mantle over your shoulders, and kiss you forever. You didn't deny me on that first evening. Remove this wrap.'

She held back my hand gently, but firmly. On her lips blossomed a mysterious smile, and she shook her head.

'Not today? Why?'

Again silence and that same prohibitive head movement.

'Why are you silent? Do you know that so far you

haven't exchanged a word with me? Say something! I want to hear your voice – it has to be sweet and resonant like the sound of expensive crystal.'

Jadwiga said nothing. A deep sadness had spread over her entire face, chilling the entrancing moment. Was she speechless?

So I stopped insisting, and in silence I was already taking in her divine body. Today she was even more passionate than at our last meeting. Every so often a lustful spasm seized her – her eyes misted over with swooning, her face turned a deathly pale, her delicate, silky skin twitched, her pearly teeth grated painfully. Then, terrified, I would let her go and try to revive her. But all of this was just a momentary occurrence; her paroxysm would pass quickly, and a new wave of passion – young, impulsive, totally unrestrained – would plunge us into the depths of frenzy . . . .

We parted company late at night, at about one. Upon our farewell, she pinned a small bouquet of violets to my person. I raised her hand to my lips:

'Again in a week?'

She nodded her head.

'Let it be so. Good-bye, *Carissima*!'

I went out.

While putting on my coat in the antechamber, I remembered the cigarette case I had placed on the console table. I immediately returned to the room to retrieve it.

'Excuse me,' I began, turning to where I had left Jadwiga a moment ago.

But the phrase died on my lips. Jadwiga was not in the bedroom. Had she already gone to the adjoining room? Yet this did not seem possible, for I had not heard the sound of a door opening.

'Hmm, peculiar,' I muttered, putting away my cigarette case, 'most peculiar . . . .'

And slowly, lost in thought, I went down the steps and out onto the street.

*　　　*　　　*

My relationship with Jadwiga Kalergis has now gone on for several months, still wrapped in complete secrecy before the world. No one imagines that I am the lover of the most beautiful woman in town. So far no one has seen us together in public. I would even suppose that people know nothing of her return. At least that's the impression I've received from chance conversations with my circle of acquaintances. This is a little strange, but it seems Jadwiga had returned stealthily, not desiring that it be known at all. Perhaps she has some hidden reason, which she does not wish to reveal to me. I do not press her on this matter and know how to behave discreetly.

In general, my mistress is a strange woman, and she likes to surround herself in mystery. I still have to get used to her whimsicality and accommodate her eccentric habits; I continually find in her behaviour something incomprehensible. Though we have been with each other for half a year, as yet I haven't heard her voice. In the first few weeks I repeatedly insisted on a reason for this. In answer came letters the day after our meetings requesting that I do not ask her about it, that I stop unnecessarily tormenting her, and so on. Finally I gave up. Maybe she had suffered some injury and has really lost the ability to speak? Now it's an embarrassment to her, and instead of acknowledging her disability, maybe she prefers to leave me in doubt as to its cause?

We still see each other only once a week and always on a Saturday – she doesn't receive me on any other day. Here I must mention the strange beginning of every such visit.

When I enter the bedroom, I do not always find her there. Sometimes I have to wait a long time before she comes out to greet me. And she always does this so unnoticeably, so quietly, that I never know when and from where she emerges. Usually she stops right behind me and kisses me on the neck. Her kiss is delightful, sweet – but terrible as well. Besides, I have a feeling that I am never in a completely normal state at that moment. What type of state it is, I am not able to say — maybe some light reverie or entrancement?

In any event, whenever Jadwiga keeps me waiting a long time, I feel an overpowering urge to gaze at the Greek shield. A thought comes to me, from where I do not know, that the shield was placed there deliberately to draw attention to itself and fix one's eyes on its brilliant circles. Who knows whether it is not, in fact, the cause of that strange state into which I sometimes fall?

Later, after this prelude, everything proceeds along normally: we are eager for each other, we caress each other, we even play tricks and jokes on each other. But the beginning is always as I have described it — a little strange . . . .

One other circumstance doesn't completely satisfy me — actually something quite minor, yet unwelcome. Jadwiga likes covering her head to excess with a type of Greek veil of a dazzling white, close-knit fabric. I detest this veil! If she would merely cover her hair and the back of her head — but, besides this, she repeatedly covers her alabaster forehead, she jealously hides a portion of her face, conceals her lips, her eyes . . . .

When I want to remove this milky veil, she seems to get angry and escapes to the far corner of the room. What obstinacy! But it is said that beautiful women are like chimeras. One has to know how to accommodate them. Yet sometimes I cannot control myself. Irritated the last time by this rather eastern custom, reminiscent of a masquerade, I grabbed her as she tried to slip away. My movement was rough and clumsy: I tore her costly snow-white peplos, of which a large section remained in my hand. I put it away for a memento and always carry it with me.

*   *   *

The other day, on Saturday, I made a strange observation. As usual, when I entered the villa in the evening I did not find Jadwiga in the bedroom. I avoided glancing at the Medusa on the shield and went to the niche separated from the rest of the room by a long white curtain hanging down from a brass rod. Suddenly I noticed that the curtain bore signs of being torn; near the middle was a semi-circular gap. I mechanically took the material in my hand and began to pass it through my fingers. The fabric's softness and silkiness were somehow familiar. Involuntarily I reached into my pocket and took out the peplos fragment I had concealed as a memento. I compared its shape to the outline created by the torn-off portion of the curtain. A strange thought occurred to me: they seemed identical. I placed the section in my hand to the curtain's torn edges. Most interesting! The fragment filled the gap exactly! As if it were not torn from the dress but from the curtain, or as if the peplos and the curtain were one and the same.

Greeting Jadwiga a half hour later, I paid close attention to her dress. Any signs of it having been torn were gone; the garment fell to her feet in immaculate folds, untainted by the slightest flaw. She evidently noticed my observation because she smiled half-playfully, half-mysteriously. I then raised the torn peplos piece and led her to the niche to show her what I had seen. A strange thing, however! The curtain was not there! A funny thought suggested itself: Had she 'borrowed' it for her peplos?

Meanwhile, instead of the curtain, the arms of a sheltered recess opened up invitingly before us. I glanced at Jadwiga. She responded with a smile of bewitching encouragement . . . .

*   *   *

Not long ago I made an interesting discovery. Jadwiga has birthmarks that are exactly identical to my own. A funny coincidence! The more amusing in that these marks even appear in the same places. A dark-red one, shaped like a bunch of grapes and the size of a nut, on the right shoulder-blade, and the second one, a mole high up on the left groin. The chance resemblance of these physical details intrigues me, the more so as these marks do not have typical features – on the contrary, they have a strongly individualized character. Peculiar, isn't it?

I have noticed something else. Her skin, particularly on the chest and shoulders, has a darkish tinge, as if from repeated sun tanning. The same is true of me. I acquired this epidermal feature through many summers of sun-bathing. Can one explain it in the same way for her? I doubt it. As far as I know she avoids the sun and pulls down the blinds in her mansion to bar its rays. I, on the other hand, like the sunlight immensely, and allow it to pass through my window as much as possible.

*   *   *

Jadwiga's eccentricities definitely exceed all limits. For several weeks she has been receiving me in a half-lit, sometimes dim room and forces me to wait for hours. When she finally emerges from some dark corner, she is completely wrapped in those loathsome veils, so that at times she creates the impression of an apparition. Last week she gazed at me from behind these coverings as if through a narrow slit.

Yet, at the same time, her passion has increased. That woman is going mad! She has wound herself up in a vicious sexual circle, and she rolls about licentiously, writhing in lustful convulsions. There are moments when I cannot keep up with her satanic pace, and I am left behind dazed, exhausted, breathless. Damn! I hadn't really known Jadwiga Kalergis!

On the other hand, I have observed in her figure something quite unique, something that one might define as 'elusiveness.' Whether it's due to those white coverings in which she now carefully wraps herself, or whether it's a consequence of the inadequate lighting – at moments her figure evades my sight. Interesting illusions and optical surprises arise from this. At times I see her doubly, at other times as if strangely diminished – then again, as if from a distance. Absolutely like a 'dance of the seven veils' or a cubist painting. Frequently she looks like a statue not completely carved, in some enigmatic stage of formation – a sort of half-finished project.

And that 'elusiveness' also crosses over into the tactile sphere. Particularly as it concerns the upper portion of her body. Several times I have ascertained with dismay that her shoulders and chest, not long ago so compact and limber, are now strangely limp. Under the pressure of my hand, her dress recedes somewhere inside, and I am unable to feel the former resilience of her body.

One night, intensely irritated by this and seized by an overwhelming urge, I suddenly decided to prick her. I slowly drew out an opal pin from my cravat and plunged it into her naked leg. Blood squirted out, and a cry was heard – but from my lips: at that moment I felt a sharp pain in my leg. Jadwiga was looking with a peculiar smile at the blood dripping from her wound in large ruby drops. Not a word of complaint came from her lips.

Returning home late that night, I had to change my clothing, for it was stained in blood. To this day I carry a mark on my leg from that pin prick.

★　　　★　　　★

I will not go there anymore! After what happened at The Lindens on the last Saturday of August, a month ago, life has lost its attraction for me. My hair has turned white overnight. My acquaintances cannot recognize me when they see me on the street. Apparently I was laid up senseless for a week, raving as if in a fever. Today I went out for the first time. I wobble like an old man and support myself on a walking stick. A horrible end! . . .

It happened on August 28th, not quite a year since the start of that ill-fated relationship.

That evening I was late. Some pressing review or literary article occupied me two extra hours: I arrived at eight.

The bedroom was dark. I stumbled against the furniture a few times, and a little irritated by this, I said loudly:

'Good evening, Jadwiga! Why haven't you put on the lights? One can break one's neck in this darkness!'

I received no answer. Not the slightest movement betrayed her presence. Nervously, I started to look for some matches. Apparently my intention did not please her, for suddenly I felt something cool brush my cheek, as if from a hand, and I heard a soft, barely perceptible whisper:

'Don't put on the lights. Come to me, Jerzy! I am in the niche.'

I shuddered, perturbed by an odd sensation. For the first time since we had been together I heard her voice – in truth, her whisper. Groping, I advanced toward the bed. The whisper died and did not return. I did not see her face, for the darkness was almost complete; only some indistinct whiteness was visible. She must have been already in her underclothing. I stretched out my hand to clasp her and encountered her naked hips. A thrill ran through my body, and my blood seethed. In a moment I was already taking in the sweetness of her womanhood. She was insane. The giddy scent of her body intoxicated my senses and incited a craving to possess her completely. The passionate rhythm of her divine hips inflamed my blood and drove me wild. But I sought her lips without success, I tried to enclose her in my arms to no avail. I began to pass my trembling hands about the pillow, to slide them along the length of her body. I met only wraps, veils. She had, as it were, completely enclosed herself in the fire of her sex, withdrawing everything except that. Finally I lost all patience. Feelings of wounded pride, lowered dignity, rose in fervent opposition. I had to have her lips at all costs. Why was she denying me them? Didn't I have a right to them?

Suddenly I remembered that nearby on the wall was an electric switch. Kneeling on the bed, I found the lever with my fingers and flipped it up. The light gushed, illuminating the room. I looked down and, propelled by boundless terror, jumped out of bed.

Before me, in a turmoil of lace and satin, lay the bare, shamelessly spread-out body of a woman – a body without breasts, without shoulders, without a head . . . .

With a cry of dread, I rushed out of the bedroom; I leapt like a madman down the stairs and found myself in the street. In the quiet night, I hurried along the bridge . . . .

In the morning, I was found unconscious on a garden bench.

*   *   *

Two months later, passing The Lindens by chance, I noticed workmen in the park. Roses were being wrapped in straw coverings for the winter. An elegantly dressed man was emerging from an alley, speaking to someone.

Seized by an irresistible urge, I approached him, tipping my hat:

'Excuse me. Is this the house of Jadwiga Kalergis?'

'At one time it was her's,' came the answer. 'A week ago her family took possession of their inheritance.'

I felt a strange tightness in my throat.

'Inheritance?' I asked, straining for an indifferent tone.

'Why, yes. Jadwiga Kalergis has been dead for two years. She was killed in a hiking accident in the Alps. Sir, what's wrong? You've turned pale.'

'Nothing – nothing at all. Sorry to have bothered you. Thank you for the information.'

Tottering, I went along the shore to the city . . . .

THE WANDERING TRAIN

Feverish activity reigned at the Horsk train station. It was right before the holidays, an eagerly anticipated time when people could take off from work for a few days. The platform swarmed with those arriving and departing. Women's excited faces flashed by, colourful hat ribbons flapped around, frantic rushing marked every scene. Here, the slender cylinder of an elegant gentleman's top hat pushed through the crowds; there, a priest's black cassock could be seen; elsewhere, under arcades, soldiers in blue squeezed through the crush; nearby, workers in their grey shirts tried to make their way in the press.

Exuberant life seethed and overflowed noisily beyond the confines of the station. The chaotic bustle of the passengers, the exhortations of the porters, the sound of whistles, the noise of released steam all merged into a giddy symphony in which one became lost, surrendering the diminished, deafened self onto the waves of a mighty element to be carried, rocked, dazed . . . .

The railway employees were working at a quick pace. Traffic officials, standing out in their red caps, appeared everywhere – giving orders, clearing the absentminded from the tracks, and passing a swift, vigilant eye on trains at their moment of departure. Conductors were in a constant rush, walking with speedy steps through the lengthy coaches. Signalmen gave concise yet effective instructions – commands for departure. Everything went along at a brisk tempo, marked off to the minute, to the second – everyone's eyes were involuntarily checking the time on the white double-dial clock above.

Yet a quiet spectator standing to the side would have, after a brief observation, received impressions incompatible with the ostensible order of things.

Something had slipped into the standard regulations and traditional course of activities; some type of undefined, though weighty obstacle opposed the sacred smoothness of rail travel.

One could deduce this from the nervous, exaggerated gestures of the railwaymen and their restless glances and anticipating faces. Something had broken down in the previously exemplary system. Some unhealthy, terrible current circulated along its hundredfold-branched arteries, and it permeated to the surface in half-conscious flashes.

The zeal of the railwaymen reflected their obvious willingness to overcome whatever had stealthily wormed its way into a perfect structure. Everyone was in two or three places at once to forcefully suppress this irritating nightmare, to subordinate it to the regular demands of work, to the wearisome but safe equilibrium of routine chores.

This was, after all, their area, their 'region,' exercised through many years of diligent application, a terrain which, it seemed, they knew through and through. They were, after all, exponents of that sphere of practical work where to them, the initiated, nothing should be unclear, where they, the representatives and sole interpreters of the entire complicated train system, could not and should not be caught unawares by any type of enigma. Why, for a long time everything had been calculated, weighed, measured – everything, though complex, had not passed human understanding – and everywhere there was a precise moderation without surprises, a regularity of repeated occurrences foreseen from the start!

They felt, then, a collective responsibility toward the great mass of the travelling public to whom was owed complete peace and safety.

Meanwhile their inner perplexity, flowing in vexatious waves over the passengers, was picked up by the public.

If it had at least concerned a so-called 'accident,' which, admittedly, one couldn't foresee but which later on, after its occurrence, could be somehow explained – certainly against an accident even they, the professionals, were helpless but not desperate. But something totally different was at issue here.

Something incalculable like a chimera, capricious like madness had arrived, and it shattered with one blow the traditional arrangement of things.

Therefore, they felt ashamed of themselves and humiliated before the public.

At present it was most important that the problem should not spread, that 'the general public' should not find out anything about it. It was appropriate to conceal any counter-measures so that this strange affair would not come to light in the newspapers and create a public uproar.

So far the secret had been miraculously confined to the circle of the railwaymen. A truly amazing solidarity united these people: they were silent. They communicated with each other by telling glances, specific gestures, and a play on well-chosen words. Thus far the public did not know anything about any problem.

And 'the problem' was indeed strange and puzzling.

For a certain time there had appeared on the nation's railways a train not included in any known register, not entered in the count of circulating locomotives – in a word, an intruder without patent or sanction. One couldn't even state what category it belonged to or from what factory it had originated, as the brief space of time it allowed itself to be seen made any determination in this respect impossible. In any event, judging by the incredible speed with which it moved before the dumbfounded eyes of onlookers, it had to occupy a very high standing among trains: at the very least it was an express.

Yet most distressing was its unpredictability. The intruder turned up everywhere, suddenly appearing from some railway line to fly by with a devilish roar along the tracks before disappearing in the distance. One day it had been seen near the station at M.; the following day it appeared in an open field beyond the town of W.; a couple of days later it flew by with petrifying impudence near a lineman's booth in the district of G.

At first it was thought that the insane train belonged to an existing line and that only tardiness or a mistake by the officials concerned had failed to ascertain its identity. Therefore, inquiries began, endless signalling and communications between stations – all to no avail: the intruder simply sneered at the endeavours of the officials, usually appearing where it was least expected.

Particularly disheartening was the circumstance that nowhere could one catch, overtake or stop it. Several planned pursuits to this end on one of the most technologically advanced engines created a horrible fiasco: the terrible train immediately took the lead.

Then the railway personnel began to be seized by a superstitious fear and a stifled rage. An unheard of thing! For quite a few years the coaches and cars had run according to a established plan that had been worked out at headquarters and approved by government officials – for years everything had been able to be calculated, to be more or less foreseen, and when some 'mistake' or 'oversight' occurred, it could be understood and corrected. Then suddenly an uninvited guest slips onto the tracks, spoiling the order of things, turning regulations upside down, and bringing confusion and disarray to a well-regulated organization.

Thank goodness the interloper had not brought about any disaster. This was something which generally puzzled them from the very beginning. The train always appeared on a track which was free at the time; so far it had not caused a collision. Yet one could occur any day now. Indeed, that's where things seemed to be heading. From a role as the hunted, the intruder became the hunter, and started to directly menace the smooth running, old order of things. Unlike in the beginning when it avoided other trains, the unknown train now seemed to be getting closer to its regular-running comrades. Already it had shot by an express on its way to O.; a week ago it barely avoided a passenger train between S. and F.; the other day it was only by a miracle that it successfully avoided the express from W.

Station-masters trembled at the news of these near misses,

which had been occurring with more frequency. Only double tracks and the quick judgement of engine drivers had thus far avoided a collision. Yet the affair could end tragically any day.

For a month the station-master at Horsk had also been leading an unpleasant existence. In constant anxiety before an unexpected visit of the mysterious train, he was almost continually vigilant, not deserting by day or night the signal-box that had been entrusted to him nearly a year ago as a token of recognition for 'his energy and uncommon efficiency.' And the post was important, for the Horsk station was one of the most important and busy railway junctions in the whole country.

Today, faced with a greatly increased number of passengers, his work was particularly difficult.

Evening was slowly falling. Electric lights flashed up, reflectors threw off their powerful projections. In the green glow of junction-signals, rails started to glitter with a gloomy-metallic glaze that curved along with the cold iron serpents. Here and there, in the shadowy twilight, a conductor's lamp flickered faintly, a lineman's signal blinked. In the distance, far beyond the station, where the emerald eyes of lanterns were already being extinguished, a semaphore was making night signals.

Here, leaving its horizontal position, the arm of the semaphore rose to an angle of forty-five degrees: the passenger train from Brzesk was approaching . . . .

One could already hear the panting respiration of the locomotive, the rhythmic clatter of the wheels; one could already see the bright-yellow glass of its front. The train was heading into the station . . . .

From its open windows lean out the golden locks of children, the curious faces of women; welcoming kerchiefs are waved.

The throngs waiting on the platform push toward the coaches, outstretched hands on both sides tend toward a meeting . . . .

What kind of commotion is that to the right? Strident

whistles rend the air. The station-master is shouting something in a hoarse, wild voice.

'Away! Get back, run! Reverse steam! Backwards! Backwards! . . . Collision!!'

The masses throw themselves in a dense onrush toward the barriers, breaking them . . . . Frenzied eyes instinctively look to the right – where the railway service has gathered – and see the spasmodic, aimlessly frantic vibrations of lanterns endeavouring to turn back a train, which with its entire momentum is coming from the opposite side of the same track occupied by the Brzesk passenger train. Shrill whistles cut the desperate responses of horns and the hellish tumult of people. In vain! The unexpected locomotive is getting closer with terrifying velocity; the enormous green lights of the engine weirdly push aside the darkness, the powerful pistons move with fabulous, possessed efficiency . . . .

From a thousand breasts a horrible alarm bursts out, a cry swelled by a fathomless panic:

'It's the insane train! The madman! On the ground! Help! On the ground! We're lost! Help! We're lost!'

Some type of gigantic, grey mass passes by – an ashen, misty mass with cut-out windows from end to end; one can feel the gust of a satanic draft from these open holes, hear the flapping, maddeningly blown-about blinds; one can almost see the passengers' spectral faces . . . .

Suddenly something strange occurs. The insane train, instead of shattering its comrade, passes through it like a mist; for a moment one can see the two fronts of the trains go through each other, one can see the noiseless grazing of the coach walls, the paradoxical osmosis of gears and axles; one more second, and the intruder permeates with lightning fury through the train's solid body and disappears somewhere in the field on the other side. Everything quietens down . . . .

On the track, before the station, the intact Brzesk passenger train stands peacefully. About it, a great bottomless silence. Only from the meadows in the distance comes the low chirp of crickets, only along the wires above flows the gruff chat of the telegraph . . . .

The people on the platform, the railwaymen, the clerks rub their eyes and look about in amazement:

Had what they seen really happened or was it just a bad hallucination?

Slowly, all eyes, united in the same impulse, turn toward the Brzesk train – it continues to stand silent and still. From inside, lamps burn with a steady, quiet light, at the open windows the breeze plays gently on the curtains . . . .

A grave silence inhabits the cars; no one is disembarking, no one is leaning out from within. Through the illuminated quadrangle windows one can see the passengers: men, women and children; everyone whole, uninjured – no one has received even the most minor contusion. Yet their state is strangely puzzling . . . .

Everyone is in a standing position, facing the direction of the vanished phantom locomotive. Some terrible force has bewitched these people, holding them in dumb amazement, some strong current has polarized this assembly of souls to one side. Their outstretched hands indicate some unknown goal, an aim surely distant; their inclined bodies lean to the distance, to a stunning, misty land far away; and their eyes, glazed by wild alarm and enchantment, are lost in boundless space . . . .

So they stand and are silent; no muscle will twitch, no eyelid will fall. So they stand and are silent . . . .

Because through them has passed a most strange breath, because they have been touched by a great awakening, because they are already . . . insane . . . .

Suddenly strong and familiar sounds were heard, wrapped in the security of the familiar – strokes as firm as a heart when it beats against a healthy chest – steady sounds of habit, for years proclaiming the same thing . . . .

'Ding-dong' – and a pause – 'ding-dong . . . ding-dong . . .'

The signals were operating . . . .

STRABISMUS

He had attached himself to me, I don't know how or when.

His name was Brzechwa, Jozef Brzechwa. What a name! Something about it fastens and hooks onto the nerves, irritating them with its grating resonance. He was cross-eyed. He especially saw poorly out of his right eye, which peered out in a stone gaze under ruddy lashes. His small, brick-coloured face grimaced perpetually in a malicious sneer of half-irony, as if in this sorry way it could avenge its own ugliness and squalor. A tiny, rusty moustache, twirled rakishly upward, moved constantly, like the pincers of a poisonous scarabaeus – sharp, stinging, evil.

A horrible man.

He was agile, elastic as a ball, slender-figured, of medium build; he walked with a light, elusive step and could slip into a room without being noticed.

I couldn't stand him from the first time I saw him, and felt an indescribable disgust whenever I looked at him, particularly as his physical features suited his character.

This person was extremely different from me in his disposition, tastes and behaviour. That is why I felt such a strong antipathy towards him. He was my living antithesis, with whom there could be no reconciliation. Maybe precisely because of this he latched himself onto me with a rabid passion, as if sensing my natural aversion toward him.

He probably experienced particular delight in seeing how unsuccessfully I tried to extricate myself from the nets he was always ensnaring me with. He was my inseparable companion in cafés, on walks, at the club; he knew how to worm his way into the circles of my nearest acquaintances; what's more, he could conquer the favour of women to whom I was closely connected. He knew of my smallest plans, my slightest movements.

More than once, so as to be free of looking at his loathsome physiognomy for even just a single day, I would escape unseen by carriage or automobile to the outskirts of town, or else, with no prior word betraying my intention, I would set out for another locality. How can I describe my amazement when, after a while, Brzechwa would suddenly spring up, as if from under the ground, saying with a sneering sweet smile how happy he was at our unexpected, pleasant meeting!

It finally reached the point where his presence inspired a superstitious fear in me and I considered him my evil spirit or demon. His annoying cat-like movements, the cunning narrowing of his eyes, and, most of all, his strabismus, with the cold glossiness of the scleras, curdled my blood with inconceivable dread, while simultaneously stirring up boundless rage.

And he knew perfectly well the easiest way to infuriate me. He was always able to agitate my most sensitive nerves. As soon as he had discovered my tastes and what I held important, he took every opportunity to deride them so savagely that it seemed he wanted to exclude any opposition.

One point of contention fundamentally separating us was the question of individualism, which I always defended with ardent passion. I have a feeling that around this very axis revolved our entire antagonism.

I was a staunch admirer of everything personal, original, unique, self-contained. Brzechwa, to the contrary, scoffed at every kind of individualism, considering it a chimera of presumptuous fools. Hence, he didn't believe in any inventiveness or ingeniousness, reducing them to the influences of environment, race, the 'spirit of the times,' and so on.

'I even believe,' he would drawl more than once, criss-crossing his eyes in my direction, 'that each one of us contain several individuals who fight for that worthless scrap, the so-called "soul." '

This obvious banter was meant to elicit a passionate reaction on my part. Realizing this, I would pretend that I hadn't heard anything and ignore him. Then he would be on the lookout for another opportunity to pronounce his 'collective position,' as he termed it.

Whenever I displayed admiration and rapture for some new work of art or scientific invention, Brzechwa, with cynical calm, would attempt to prove the groundlessness of my adoration, or else he would silently sit opposite me and transfix me with his frightful strabismus, a smile of malicious sarcasm never leaving his open lips.

He didn't feel any aesthetic thrills at all: beauty didn't act upon him in any sense of the word. Instead, he was a sports enthusiast. There wasn't an automobile race, a cycling competition or soccer match in which he didn't shine. He fenced like a master, was a great shot, and had the reputation of being a first-class swimmer. Education and scholars he ignored, holding to the maxim *nihil novi sub sole*. Despite this, one couldn't deny his great intelligence, which showed itself in witty and vitriolic sayings. Of a hot-headed nature, he was unable to endure opposition, and had continual rows and countless affairs of honour, from which he always emerged successful.

A strange thing, however: he was never offended by anything I said, however uncivil or insulting my words. I alone had the privilege of insulting him. Apparently he saw this as my due for his never-ending sneering and pestering. Perhaps there was another reason – but what, I don't know.

Sometimes I would intentionally exaggerate to goad him into a serious quarrel that would end our relationship. A fruitless activity. Sensing what was happening, he would dismiss my moral condemnation with his very sweet smile and turn everything into a joke . . . .

Finally I got rid of him. An event occurred that seemed, once and for all, to liberate me from his clutches. He died a sudden, violent death, and I was the indirect cause.

One day, at the end of my tether, I struck him in the face. Brzechwa instantly bridled. He turned white as a sheet, and then I caught sight of a steely flash in his eyes that I had never seen before. He quickly hid his anger, however, and laid a shaking hand on my shoulder.

'You got unnecessarily carried away,' he said with a tremulous voice. 'It's to no avail. Neither you nor I are capable of offending the other. You see, my dear sir, it is exactly as if someone wanted to slap his own face. Both of us are really one.'

'Bastard!' I muttered through my teeth.

'As you please. This will not change a thing.'

And his eyes began to criss-cross like crazy.

The row had, nevertheless, a serious, tragic consequence for him. Since everything had occurred in the presence of several witnesses, people found out about the incident and from then on no one granted him the freedom to do as he pleased. Brzechwa flew into rages, arranged scandalous 'practical jokes,' and eventually forced one of his greatest enemies to an encounter with revolvers. Even though my argument with him had set up the basis for such an event, Brzechwa asked me to be his second. I refused, and though I didn't care for Brzechwa's opponent, I offered my services to him. I did this intentionally, pleased that, at least obliquely, I could do away with my persecutor. My offer was accepted, and the duel, under very strict conditions, took place in a grove on the outskirts of the city. Brzechwa fell, shot in the forehead.

I remember his last glance: it was directed at me, a piercing look that paralyzed the will. Immediately afterwards he ceased breathing. I left, not daring to look any longer at that demonic, twisted face. But that face will never disappear from my memory; it is deeply etched there in indelible lines, and that terrible strabismus will eternally gash my soul with its cross-eyed stare.

Brzechwa's death, particularly the last painful moments of his life, upset me so strongly that shortly afterwards I came down with a severe brain fever. The illness dragged on for months, and when – thanks to the untiring help of doctors and amid constant anxiety about a relapse – I finally got well, I was unrecognizable. My character was completely altered; it seemed alien, and even antagonistic, to the person I had been before. My former tastes, my noble fervour for everything beautiful and profound, my refined faculty for perceiving a flicker of originality were now gone. There only remained – an enigmatic detail – the memory that I had once possessed these virtues.

I became a practical person, 'healthy,' normal to the point of nausea, an enemy of any type of eccentricity – and the most painful thing for me – I started to sneer at my former ideals. My every word and gesture was clothed in sarcasm or malicious laughter; everything I did seemed false.

Aware of these new changes within me, I attempted to somehow resist. So began a fierce struggle between two different selves, of whose coexistence I was deeply convinced. But the new self always prevailed, and despite my inner loathing I always listened to his promptings.

It was like the difference between theory and practice. In my principles I remained the same as always and with indignation watched the actions of the other me, who had like a thief slipped into my innermost core and was getting rid of what had been my essence, replacing it with his vileness.

And I wouldn't describe my condition as the commonly-known 'split personality,' for what had occurred was a completely different matter that could not be psychologically explained by the first half of my life. I felt that one couldn't speak of a splitting of oneself, rather of a doubling up. It was as if some diabolic intruder had moved in. I carried him within, continually wounding myself with this horrid coexistence, powerless, despairing over the awareness of a change I couldn't dismiss. Each one of my deeds aroused an inner opposition and represented itself as a will imposed on me from outside; each word was a lie unsupported by conviction, devoid of the strength of feelings. Worse still, the intruder encroached into the domain of my thoughts and beliefs, trying to reshape me completely in his own image.

Whenever I wanted to behave in a manner consistent with my former attitude toward the world, some strong force from within me would compel me to the new, unbearable path, and I would hear a snigger inside me and see in my mind's eye a devilish strabismus . . . .

I detested myself both physically and morally. I couldn't stand my own being because it seemed disgusting, grotesque.

So as to reduce the antics of the new 'I' to a tolerable minimum, I shut myself up at home for days on end and avoided people, in whose eyes I saw both amazement and aversion.

Here in my quiet abode, in a secluded quarter of the city, I passed long hours of torment, struggling with my hidden enemy. Here within four silent walls I spent long moments thinking about my internal agony.

In due course in my struggle with the intruder, I achieved a certain skill in excluding him, at least for a brief time, from the process of my thinking. Total isolation, freedom from the hustle and bustle allowed me, even if only for a couple of minutes, to focus my attention on my real, former self and liberate it from the brutal iron hand of the usurper.

These were truly great efforts. I had the impression of a person who, with titanic strength, separates two heavy half-globes and succeeds in keeping them apart for a few moments.

Then, taking advantage of such occasions, I threw myself into my writing and filled up page after page with the thoughts that had been seething inside me but which couldn't find an outlet, for they had been suppressed by my other self. With bated breath, I wrote like a madman, driving my hand across the paper to express what I thought and felt, to state before the world that I am not the person I will appear to be in an hour or a few minutes' time.

But this frantic effort never lasted long. All that was needed was a shout from the street, the entrance of a servant into the room, or the sight of a passerby's face, and my tense nerves would split like cords, my taut muscles would snap with a dull crack, and the obstinate half-globes would press together to form a hermetically sealed, uniform sphere. A horrible, cynical laugh would issue from my lips, and sobbing with anguish, I would thoroughly destroy whatever I had written.

And once again I'd return to the outside world, disgracefully changed to a base, sneering individual without any values and beliefs. And once again long exertions of thought would be necessary, withdrawal from the world and absolute solitude, so that I could, even if only for a couple of minutes, isolate myself from the incursions of that hateful being and exclude him from my soul.

Yet in repeating these experiences I achieved increasingly encouraging results. For longer periods I was able to hold myself apart from the alien intruder and to cleanse myself of his filth.

Afterwards, of course, everything reverted to the previous state, but the memory of these short liberations stimulated further attempts. Eventually I became myself for a couple of hours, and I took advantage of this in the best possible manner, hurrying before my enemy would return.

But constant observation and guarding of oneself at every step, a necessity for this mental electrolysis of the doubled 'I,' wearied me extremely, making me nervous and leaving me with violent headaches.

Nevertheless, having acquired a dim hope of reclaiming my true being, I didn't spare myself and already dreamt of the moment I could freely appear as my own person in company . . . .

One day, after a longer stay in the world, I shut myself in for a specific aim and undertook the arduous work of separation. As a result of practice this task was easier, and I soon inhabited my own being again. I turned my attention to my immediate physical surroundings so that, under this new condition, I could get accustomed to maintaining a measure of control over my individuality, eventually doing so in the face of the hundredfold stronger distractions of the world.

As I was slowly moving away from self-concentration and absentmindedly glancing about the room, I thought I heard some noise beyond the left wall. Curious, I began to listen, but this directed me too strongly to the outside, bringing about the fatal merging of barely separated elements, and again I stopped being myself.

Brokenhearted, I cursed the suspicious noise, which, anyway, might only have been an illusion of wandering thoughts caused by nervous tension. Thus my first attempt at reclaiming myself while being attentive to my surroundings proved abortive. Nevertheless, I didn't lose hope, and a couple of days later I conducted a test . . . .

As long as I was preoccupied with myself, I didn't hear anything suspicious beyond the wall – but as soon as I started to pay more attention to my surroundings, I heard that same mysterious noise coming from the left side. Even though I knew perfectly well that as a consequence I would lose myself and return to that loathsome double existence, I immediately thrust my head out of the window and glanced to the left with the hope of discovering the cause of this noise.

The house I lived in had one storey and consisted of three sections. I occupied the end wing, so that beyond me on the left side were no more rooms, and the outer wall faced a small, enclosed garden. As usual at that time no one was in it; generally, no one came up on my side, respecting my privacy and discreetly avoiding the line of my windows.

Uneasy, I drew my head back inside.

It occurred to me that perhaps the puzzling noise had been accompanying the cleansing process of the self for some time. Very likely, taken up with intense internal work and projecting it onto paper, I hadn't noticed what had been happening around me. Only when I had pulled back a certain distance from my newly crystallized individuality and turned my attention to my surroundings had I been able to detect these mysterious sounds. Though I wasn't sure why this was happening during my attempts at spiritual emancipation, I eventually had to admit to a connection, because the noise made itself heard only when I succeeded in casting off my hateful fetters.

Frequently, when I was in my usual double state, I would listen for something to reach me from that side – but to no avail: the wall at those times didn't let through the slightest tremor.

Sometimes I thought I was succumbing to an acoustic illusion and that the noise was in reality coming from the right wall, behind which lived a quiet bachelor. But this speculation was rejected after scrupulous evaluation of the sounds . . . .

Therefore the noise was coming only from beyond the left wall, beyond a wall that bordered on empty space. Most strange!

After a while, when the sounds persisted, I began to carefully examine the left wall. Soon I came to the opinion that there was a cavity inside, because when I banged it, the wall emitted a hollow reverberation.

This assumption was subsequently strengthened by a detail observed on the outside of the house. Scrutinizing attentively the left wing, I noticed for the first time, with no little surprise, that the distance between the boundary of the wall and the last window amounted to four metres. Since the wall on the inside was separated from the window by at most a metre, then its thickness was three metres, an unusual dimension for a house of this sort. Beyond me, then, was a walled-up room. And that particular noise originated from it. This was obvious.

Amazed at this discovery, for a long time I practically never left my home, spending hours on end in trying to reach my true self. Now, however, this proved to be more difficult because, catching sounds from the void, I diverted my attention too quickly from my own being. Realizing that by this road I wouldn't attain my goal, I concentrated my entire energy on thinking of myself, and only when I felt the strong intensity of my regained individuality did I listen to those sounds which emanated from the hidden room.

After a while I noticed they contained rather audible semi-tones, like gradations. The deeper I would sink into the process of my spiritual liberation and the more I would purge myself of my other self – the more distinctly the noise would make itself heard. Something restless was tramping inside that enclosed space, roaming about the corners, wandering along the length of the walls as if in frantic helplessness.

But when I was trapped again in that unhappy double state, more strongly restrained by the co-presence of the alien element, the sounds beyond the wall calmed down and faded away, as if soothed.

There was something puzzling about this, something that stimulated my utmost curiosity while evoking ice-cold fear. One had the impression that while I was here dealing with my hated enemy, endeavouring to oust him from my unfortunate ego, there, beyond the wall, some entity was being born, something was being formed, was emerging .... Finally I decided to smash down the wall and see what was inside that hidden room.

It was appropriate, however, to proceed systematically and slowly, so as not to scare away the strange being. Whenever I listened at length to the particular details of its movements, everything ceased, and I – a thing for me incomprehensible – would burst out with devilish laughter and return to my double state.

'This is some cunning beast,' I muttered, quietening down after these unexpected outbursts. 'However, we will find even for this a remedy; we will find it, and it will be infallible. One has to catch you off guard.'

I soon proceeded with my plan. I took a piece of chalk and drew on the wall a quadrangle corresponding, more or less, to my size. Then I chipped off the plaster within the marked boundaries, after which I carefully cut out with a sharp tool the inside section of the wall, leaving only a thin layer, which according to my estimate would give way with one blow.

After finishing these preparations during the day, I decided to break into the room that very evening and catch whatever had been unsettling me for many weeks.

Outside the autumn weather was typically foul; a light rain fell continually. An early dusk unreeled grey lines of curled mist along narrow suburban back-streets. From sparsely scattered lanterns spread out golden, flickering trails, dying in the distended watery expanse. Some kind of carts, wet, slippery, dragged along the road in a clattering file . . . .

I lowered the blind and lit a lamp.

I felt strange and not myself. I dropped my weary head onto my hands and sank into the work of liberation. As usual, I reminded myself of my former character, its development and its tastes; I immersed myself in drawing out my experiences before my illness; I imagined myself in typical situations in which my individuality had manifested itself most clearly. Thus I went further and further, going down ever deeper to reach the most primary layers of my ego . . . .

I was happy; I was that former self, full of belief and confidence in the future, infused with the love of goodness and beauty, fascinated by life and its secret wonders. I was at the peak of my emancipation, without a particle of alien matter, with the cleanest ego . . . .

Suddenly I looked around, taking in the room with a quick glance. At that moment a noise to my left pierced my solitude. Something was hurling itself around beyond the wall, as if from the floor to the ceiling, scraping along the walls in despair, rolling around in painful fits, without finding a way out . . . .

I listened with bated breath, clenching a pick in my hand. After several minutes the noise quietened down; fretful, nervous steps followed. Someone, clearly of this world, was pacing up and down in that hidden room, from corner to corner.

I raised the pick and with all my strength hit the marked wall . . . .

I rushed inside, and at that moment came a deadly silence.

I was hit with the stifling, putrid odour of a sealed space.

At first, stunned by the blinding darkness, I saw nothing. But a long streak of light from my lamp slipped into the void after me, and it crept along the floor to the corner . . . .

I looked there and let go of the pick, horror-struck.

At the corner of the little room, squeezed between two walls, crouched some human figure, staring at me with a piercing, greenish look. Drawn by the magnetic power of his gaze, I advanced . . . . The figure straightened up, grew . . . . I cried out. It was Brzechwa . . . .

He stood silent and still; only his moustache twitched slightly. Suddenly he inclined himself in my direction, leaned against my chest, and – entered me, vanishing inside without a trace . . . .

Dazed, like an automaton I went and grabbed the lamp from the table and rushed back through the breach. In vain. The room was empty. Under the ceiling swung cobwebs, along the walls trickled cold tears of humidity . . . .

Suddenly a sound cut the air, hoarse, whizzing, grating . . . .

'What's that?! What's that?!'

Then I realized: it was my laughter.

VENGEANCE OF THE ELEMENTALS

Antoni Czarnocki, the fire chief of Rakszawa, had just finished his study of fire statistics, and lighting his favourite Cuban cigar, he stretched himself out on the ottoman.

It was three o'clock on a scorching July afternoon. Through the lowered blinds, dark-yellow daylight trickled, invisible waves of humid heat permeated. The distant noise of the street flowed in, languid from the hot weather; lethargic flies buzzed on the windows with a faint, fitful rattle. Czarnocki pondered over the dates he had been looking at, mentally arranging the notes collected through the years, as he came to his conclusions.

No one can imagine what interesting results can be obtained with a skilful and methodical – and, of course, a highly attentive – study of fire statistics. No one would believe how much interesting material can be extracted from these dry, seemingly useless dates, how many strange, sometimes amusingly strange, manifestations one can notice in this chaos of facts apparently so similar, so monotonously repetitive.

But to search it out, to detect something of the sort – for this a special sense is needed, which few acquire; one needs a 'nose' for it, maybe even the constitution. Czarnocki certainly belonged to such an exceptional group and was aware of that fact.

He had been occupied with fire for many years, studying the element in Rakszawa and elsewhere, making exceedingly precise notes based on newspaper accounts, reading special works, perusing an immense quantity of pertinent data.

Of no small help in this original research were the meticulous maps of practically all areas of the country, and even beyond, which filled his library shelves. Amongst these were plans of cities and towns with their entire labyrinth of streets, back-streets, plazas, alleys, gardens, parks, squares, buildings, churches, tenements, plans so pedantically scrupulous that a person visiting a particular area for the first time could, with the help of these guides, move about freely and with ease, as if in his own home. Everything was numbered most thoroughly, arranged according to districts and regions, and waiting their owner's use. All he needed to do was stretch out his hand – and rectangular and square canvases, oil-skins or papers would obediently spread out before him, acquainting him with their details and peculiarities.

Czarnocki frequently spent hours devouring these maps, studying the distribution of houses and streets, comparing the planimetry of cities. It was very laborious work, demanding much patience; not always was the outcome readily known and frequently one had to wait a long time for some positive result. Yet Czarnocki wasn't easily discouraged. Noticing a suspicious detail, he would grab it in indignation, as if with pincers, and wouldn't let go until he discovered a fire that had occurred years ago, or until a fire would occur and confirm his suspicions.

The fruits of this long-standing research were the special 'fire maps' and 'fire modifications' drawn up by him. On the first were emphasized places, buildings and houses which had passed through some catastrophe, no matter if the traces of the fire were eliminated and the damage repaired, or if the fire site had been left to its own fate. The plans called 'fire modifications' underlined the changes that had occurred in the arrangement of homes and buildings as a result of a fire disaster; any shift or the slightest alteration was marked with amazing pedantry.

After the creation of both types of maps Czarnocki eventually came to some very interesting conclusions. Connecting various fire sites with lines, he became convinced that in four out of five times the fire points created outlines of strange figures. Primarily these were the shapes of short, funny beings that sometimes reminded one of child freaks, at other times, of animals – little monkeys with long, playfully turned tails, agile bow-legged squirrels, extremely hideous talapoins.

Czarnocki 'extracted' from his plans a complete gallery of these beings and, colouring them with vermilion paint, put them into his unique album titled:

Album of the Fire Elementals.

The second part of this work was *Fragments and Designs* – a multitude of grotesque figures, incomplete forms, barely developed ideas. Inside were sketches of vague heads, fragments of trunks, parts of arms and legs, segments of hairy, spread-out paws, interspersed with half-twisted figures, mangled things and tentacled growths.

Czarnocki's album seemed like the work of someone's capricious fantasy that, delighting in grotesque-diabolical beings, fills pages with multitudes of malicious, chimerical and incalculable monsters. The fire chief's collection looked like a joke, an artistic genius' florid joke which had materialized in some strange dream. But at times this caprice chilled one's blood . . . .

The second conclusion reached by this original researcher came after years of observation. Fires, he perceived, occur most frequently on Thursday. Statistics showed that in most cases this terrible element is awakened on this particular day of the week.

Czarnocki didn't think this was just coincidental. On the contrary, he found an explanation. According to him, it came from the very character of a day whose symbol is contained in its name. This day, as is known, has for ages been the day of Jove, the thunderbolt god. Not without reason do the Germanic races name the thunder day: *Donnerstag* and Thursday. And that full, precise Latin melody: *giovedi*, *jueves* and *jeudi* – do they not indicate a similar understanding?

Reaching these two important findings, Czarnocki went on to further conclusions. Philosophically learned, and clearly inclined to metaphysical speculations, he engrossed himself in his spare moments in the mystical works of early

Christianity and meditated scrupulously over various medieval tracts. The long-term study of fires and their circumstances finally led him to believe in the possible existence of previously unknown beings who, occupying some middle level between human and animal, appear beside every strong eruption of the elements.

Czarnocki found confirmation of his theories in peasant beliefs and in ancient folk tales concerning the Devil, water nymphs, gnomes, salamanders and sylphs. Today he had no doubt that elementals existed. He felt their presence at every fire and followed their maliciousness with unusual skill. Gradually this hidden and unseen world became as real to him as the human environment he belonged to. With time, he became quite familiar with the psychology of these strange creatures and their crafty, deceitful nature, and he taught himself how to neutralize and subdue this enemy. A stubborn, fully-conscious fight ensued. As Czarnocki had previously fought with fire as a blind and thoughtless element – slowly, in direct proportion to his acquaintance with its real nature, he began to look at his enemy differently. Instead of a persistent, irrational force, he gradually detected a spiteful, destructive essence that had to be reckoned with. Recently, he also perceived that his altered tactics had been noticed by the other side. At that point, the battle became more personal.

And maybe no one in the world was more qualified for this battle than Antoni Czarnocki, fire chief of Rakszawa.

His very nature, endowing him with an exceptional quality, destined him to be a conqueror of this element. The fireman's body was completely invulnerable to fire. He could stroll in the middle of the greatest conflagration, surrounded by flames, without receiving the smallest burn.

Even though his position as a fire chief didn't require him to personally fight a fire, he never spared himself and was the first to dash into the most frightful blaze. At times it seemed he was heading toward certain death, where no fireman had daring enough to go. But – wonder of wonders! – he would come back whole and healthy, a nice, slightly quizzical smile on his manly, reddened face, and after taking a breath of fresh air into his overstrained lungs, he'd return to the flames.

His compatriots paled when, with unparalleled courage, he would make his way up a blazing building, force his way through nearly burned-down porches, storm into gutted corridors and rooms.

'He's unbelievable!' whispered the firemen amongst themselves, watching their chief with both fear and awe.

Soon Czarnocki acquired the nickname 'Fireproof' and became the idol of firemen and the populace. Legends and tales began to envelop him, flavoured with wonder, from which rose some double-faced figure of the Archangel Michael and the Devil. A thousand stories circulated about him in the city, oddly interwoven with fear and adoration. Today he was commonly thought of as a good sorcerer in collusion with the world of mystery. Every movement of 'Fireproof' gave food for thought, every gesture of his took on special significance.

People were particularly amazed that the fire chief's asbestos-like characteristic seemed to spread to his clothing. At first it was thought that Czarnocki wore some unique fireproof material, a supposition quickly proven incorrect. For incidents occurred where the uncanny fire chief, caught unawares by a night alarm in wintertime, would grab hastily the first overcoat he came upon, to later emerge untouched from a fire – as usual.

Someone in a similar situation would have financially exploited such unusual gifts, but Antoni was content with people's homage and admiration. At most, he occasionally allowed himself non-profit 'experiments' done for the amazement of his co-workers or close friends. He would hold large pieces of glowing coal in his bare hand for fifteen minutes or longer, without any sign of pain; and when he threw the glowing embers back into the fire, his audience saw an unscathed hand.

No less amazing was his ability to impart his invulnerability to fire to someone else. All he had to do was momentarily hold someone's hand and that person would become impervious to fire for a while. Once, a few local doctors became obsessively interested in him, proposing several 'seances' in exchange for great remuneration. Insulted, Czarnocki rejected the offer, and for a long time ceased his informal 'experiments.'

Other, even more astounding things were related about him. A couple of firemen, who had served under him for quite a few years, swore on all that was sacred that 'Fireproof' knew how to duplicate and triplicate himself during a fire; they had spotted him in a frenzied sea of flames in several different and highly dangerous places at the same time. Christopher Slucz, a respected and trusted fireman, solemnly vouched that he had once seen at a villa's scorched bay-window three figures of Antoni, looking like triplets, flowing into a single Antoni, who then calmly went down a ladder to the ground.

How much truth there was in these tales, how much fantastic exaggeration – no one knew. What was certain was that Czarnocki was an unusual person, one who seemed born to battle with the destructive element.

Aware of his power, Czarnocki struggled with fire ever more fiercely, strengthening his attack and improving with each year the agents of combating fire.

This battle eventually became the meaning of his life; every day he pondered on more efficient means of fire prevention. Today, on this sweltering July afternoon, he had been going through his most recent notes and arranging material for his great study on fire. This would be a comprehensive work in two huge volumes, summarizing the results of his lengthy research.

And now, while smoking a fragrant Cuban cigar, he visualized the book's design and arranged the chapter sequences . . . .

Finishing his cigar, he smothered the stub in an ash tray and got up from the ottoman, a smile on his face.

'Not bad, not bad!' he murmured, pleased with his meditations. 'Everything's in order.'

Then, changing his clothes, he went to his favourite café for a game of chess . . . .

Several years passed. Antoni Czarnocki's activities took on wider range and depth. He was talked about not only in Rakszawa. The renown of 'Fireproof' grew and grew. People came from far away to see and be amazed by him. His book on fire was very popular and not just among firemen, for in a short time it saw several reprints.

But shadows also appeared. The fire chief, actively participating in fighting fires, met with several accidents during this period.

At a huge fire in a lumber warehouse in Witelowce a blazing beam unexpectedly fell, seriously injuring his right shoulder-blade. In two other fires he sustained injuries to his arm and leg from collapsing ceilings. Most recently, several weeks before Christmas, he almost lost his right hand: a heavy iron crossbar falling from a ceiling brushed against him — a few millimetres more and it would have crushed his wrist bone.

This brave man reacted to these accidents with admirable and dignified calm.

'They can't accomplish anything with fire, so they're knocking down beams,' he said, smiling nonchalantly.

Yet from that time, firemen carefully monitored his movements, not allowing him to plunge too far into a fire, particularly in places where disaster might result. Despite this, these accidents recurred with strange persistence and in situations where one least expected them. The fire chief's presence seemed to torment the spirit of destruction: quite unexpectedly, footing beams, barely severed by fire, fell in his vicinity, ceilings not yet engulfed by flames tumbled, debris the size of cannonballs dropped, and now and then big, weighty rocks, from unknown places, fell where he stood.

During these occurrences, Antoni Czarnocki just smiled gently under his moustache and continued calmly smoking his cigar. But the men operating the water pumps would carefully move away, scowling. It was becoming dangerous to be in his vicinity.

There were other concerns that no one knew about as their terrain was the very home of the fire chief.

At first one smelled a strong stench and a burning scent throughout his house; it seemed that old rags were smouldering somewhere. The horrible stink loitered in invisible waves along the corridors, oozing heavily into rooms and hanging under ceilings. Eventually the odour touched all the furniture and penetrated into clothing, underwear and the bedding. Repeated airings didn't help. Even though the doors and windows were open almost all day to the eighteen-degree cold, the disgusting smell remained. Every search to uncover its origin was to no avail; the situation was hopeless.

When, a month later, the atmosphere became tolerable, a more dangerous phenomenon arose: Czarnocki's house was overrun by fumes. For the first few days one could try and blame the servants, who might have prematurely closed the stoves. But when, despite all precautions, the stifling scent of carbon dioxide still continued, one had to look for the cause elsewhere. Changing the fuel didn't help much. Though Czarnocki now ordered wood to be burned in the stoves and forbad blocking the vents, a few members of the household got burned badly at night, and he himself woke up in the morning nauseous and with a terrible headache. Finally, unable to stay in his own home, he had to spend his nights at the house of an acquaintance.

After several weeks the fumes went away. Antoni breathed a sigh of relief and returned home.

Although he initially didn't comprehend the incidents that had visited his house so obtrusively, with time he examined their origin and understood the intention: the elementals were trying to frighten him and force him to give up the battle.

But for him this merely served to awaken the spirit of contrariness and a craving for victory.

During this time he was working on a fire-fighting

system that would surpass in effectiveness all existing ones. The extinguishing method would not be water, but rather a special gas which, spreading in thick clouds over a burning building, would absorb easily into the oxygen and smother the fire at its core.

'This will really combat fire,' he said, innocently boasting to an engineer acquaintance during a chess game. 'After my invention receives a patent, fires should cease to be so devastating.' And he twisted his moustache with satisfaction.

It was the middle of January. In perhaps two or three months, in the spring, he anticipated completing his project and sending it off to the ministry. Meanwhile he worked hard, particularly in the evening, and midnight frequently saw him bent over his plans . . . .

One day, as Marcin, an old servant in his house, was removing unburned coal from the stove, Czarnocki threw a glance at the remains and noticed something intriguing.

'Wait a moment, my good man,' he said, detaining the servant on his way out. 'Put that coal here on my desk, on the newspaper.'

Marcin, a little surprised, did as he was told.

'Yes. That's fine. You may go now.'

After the servant left, Czarnocki carefully examined the glowing embers. Since first spotting them, he had been struck by their shape. Thanks to the fire's particular capriciousness, the remains assumed the form of characters from the alphabet. In wonder he scrutinized their outlines, their finished details: perfectly sculpted from the coal were capital letters.

'An original puzzle,' he thought, playing with their arrangement in various combinations. 'Maybe something will come out of this?'

Somehow, after fifteen minutes, he got the words: FILAMENT – FLICKER – REDDEN – HYDROPHOBUS – SMOKER.

'A pleasant company,' he murmured, writing down the strange names. 'The entire fire rabble; finally I know you by name. A truly original visit, even more original than calling cards.'

Laughing, he put away his notes in a cabinet.

From then on, he had the stove remains brought to him, to discover 'mail' every time.

And the correspondence became quite interesting. After the 'preliminary introduction' came 'communications from the other dimension,' letter fragments, warnings, finally threats!

'Go away!' 'Leave us in peace!' 'Don't fool around with us!' 'You'll be sorry' – these were the words which usually ended these 'fire communications.'

For Czarnocki these admonitions gave a humorous rather than serious impression. Indeed, he rubbed his hands in satisfaction and prepared the decisive blow. He felt strong and certain of victory. The accidents that had occurred around him had stopped, and the unpleasant manifestations at his home were not being repeated.

'Instead, they're corresponding daily like good and proper friends,' he scoffed, looking over his 'fire mail' every morning. 'It seems that these little creatures can only exert their malicious energy in one direction. Now they've focused all their abilities into these "firemessages," and that's why I'm not threatened from any other side. How very fortunate. Let them write as long as possible; they'll always find in me a zealous recipient.'

But the 'correspondence' abruptly ended in the beginning of February. For a while the coal remnants still adopted the shape of letters, but despite Czarnocki's endeavours no words could be arranged; only jumbled consonants or a lengthy series of unrelated letters emerged. The 'mail' was clearly breaking down, until finally the embers lost the appearance of alphabetic characters.

'The "firemessages" are finished,' Antoni concluded, closing with a flourish his *Diary of Fire Communications*.

For several weeks there was peace. Czarnocki finished up his fire-gas project and initiated efforts at obtaining a patent. But work on his discovery had apparently tired him out, for in March he felt a considerable decline in his strength. Also, the symptoms of catalepsy appeared. He had succumbed to this condition in the past during times of nervous agitation. Now the attacks came during his sleep; awakening in the morning, he felt extremely tired, as if after a long journey. Yet he didn't fully take into account this abnormal state, for the transition to it occurred very gently, without the slightest jolt; only his sleep deepened. Along with his weariness upon awakening came a very clear and colourful memory of the journeys taken supposedly during sleep. Throughout the night he was climbing up mountains, visiting foreign cities, roaming in exotic lands. The nervous exhaustion he felt in the morning seemed directly related to his dream travels. And – a strange thing – that's the way he explained it to himself. Because for him these wanderings were completely real.

He didn't confide in anyone on this matter; as it was, people knew too much about him. Why overly reveal himself to strangers?

But if he would have paid more attention to his surroundings and what was being whispered about him, maybe even he would have been a little concerned.

Marcin, in particular, was looking at his master during this time with strange suspicion and a certain distrust.

He had good reason for this. Late one night in the first week of March, on the way from the kitchen to his little room, candle in hand, he suddenly spotted in the shadows of the corridor the quickly moving figure of his master. A little perplexed, he hurried after him, uncertain of what he had actually seen. But before he reached the end of the hallway, he saw that Czarnocki had disappeared.

Disquieted by this experience, he tiptoed to his master's chamber, where he found the fire chief fast asleep.

A couple of days later, also at night, the same thing repeated itself on the staircase. Here Marcin spotted his master leaning over the railing and staring at the bottom. His flesh crawling, the old servant rushed to the fire chief, crying:

'Sir, what are you doing? For God's sake, it's a sin!'

Before he ran up to him, the fire chief shrunk and vanished into the wall without a word of response. Making the sign of the cross, Marcin quickly went to his master's bedroom and saw that, once again, his master was fast asleep.

'What the devil!' he muttered. 'Am I seeing things? I haven't touched a drop.'

About to return to his room, he suddenly noticed a new phenomenon: several feet above the head of the sleeping man hung a flickering, blood-red fire in the shape of a flaming bush. Long, blazing tentacles shot out from this fire toward Antoni, as if trying to reach him.

'Dear God Almighty!' Marcin cried out, hurling himself with bare hands on the fiery phantom.

The flaming shrub quickly withdrew its eagerly outstretched limbs, twisted itself into a compact, uniform column of fire, and, with a silent, parting hiss, expired in a few seconds.

Darkness prevailed in a room weakly lit by the candle dropped by the servant. Czarnocki was asleep on the bed, stretched out like a board . . . .

The next day Marcin judiciously hinted something about his poor appearance and advised him to see a doctor; but Antoni dismissed him with a joke, not even sensing what was afoot.

Two weeks later the catastrophe occurred . . . .

It was the night of March 28th, a memorable night for the city. Czarnocki returned late that evening, deathly tired from a rescue action at a huge fire at some railway warehouses. He had acted like a hero and, with repeated risk to his life, saved several railwaymen who, closing themselves in a storage area, had been sleeping soundly during the conflagration. Returning around ten to his home, the fire chief, still fully clothed, threw himself on his bed and immediately sank into a deep slumber.

Concerned about his welfare for several days, Marcin kept faithful watch by a lamp in the neighbouring room, occasionally glancing into his master's chamber. Around midnight weariness overcame the old man. His grey head involuntarily rested on a table, and he dozed.

Suddenly Marcin was awakened by three knocks. He roused himself and, rubbing his eyes, listened. But the sound did not repeat itself. Then, lamp in hand, he rushed into the adjacent room.

But it was already too late. Opening the bedroom door, he saw his master in the midst of a fire whose thousand flames seemed to be invading his body.

Before the old servant could reach the bed, the fiery phantom had completely entered the sleeper.

Marcin, shaking like an aspen, looked at his master in horror.

Suddenly, Czarnocki's features underwent a strange transformation: along his motionless face passed a nervous spasm, twisting his features into a frozen grimace. Impelled by the mysterious force that had craftily taken possession of his body, the fire chief jumped up from bed and rushed out of the house with a wild cry.

It was four in the morning. Over the city stretched the final procession of sleep apparitions, reluctantly preparing for their return journey; demon ghosts sadly furled their fantastic wings, and dream angels, bending wistfully over children in bed, planted parting kisses on little foreheads . . . .

Violet light loomed on the eastern horizon. The blue-grey light of dawn flowed into the city – stirring, rousing, awakening . . . . Swarms of downtown jackdaws, wrested from sleepy stiffness, made black rings around the city-hall tower and, warbling cheerfully, perched on bare, pre-spring trees. A few stray dogs, finishing their nightly wandering amongst alleys, now sniffed for food at the marketplace . . . .

Suddenly fountains of fire shot up from several areas in the city; red, flickering curls blossomed into crimson flowers over roofs, rising to the sky. Church bells groaned; the quiet of daybreak was assailed by shouts, turmoil, voices of panic:

108

'Fire! Fire!'

Seven bloody torches lined the morning horizon, seven banners of fire unfurled themselves over the city. The Franciscan monastery was ablaze, along with the executive and justice buildings, the Church of St. Florian, the fire barracks and two private homes.

'Fire! Fire!'

Throughout the marketplace surged multitudes of people. Some person in a fireman's outfit, with windblown hair and flaming torch in hand, was feverishly pushing his way through the crowds.

'Who's that?! Who's that?! . . .'

'Stop him! Stop him!'

Ten firemen are after him.

'Grab him! Grab him! He's the arsonist!'

A thousand hands rapaciously reach out for the fugitive.

'Arsonist! Criminal!' screams the infuriated mob.

Someone knocks the torch out of his hand, someone else grabs him by his waist. He struggles and thrashes about violently, his mouth foaming . . . . Finally they subdue him. Restrained with ropes, his clothes in tatters, he is led through the square. By the pale light of dawn, people look at his face:

'Who is it?'

The hands of the firemen involuntarily withdraw.

'Who is it?'

A chill of fear breaks off sentences, stifles hoarse throats.

'Whose face is it?'

From the madman's shoulders hang the ripped epaulettes of a fire chief, on his torn jacket sparkle medals awarded for valour and distinguished service. And then there's that face – that face twisted in an animal grimace, with a pair of bloodshot, criss-crossing eyes!

For a month after the great fire, which had burned down seven of the city's most beautiful buildings, Marcin, the old servant of the Czarnocki household, saw his master's apparition sneaking into the bedchamber night after night.

The maniac's shadow stood by the empty bed and looked for its body, as if wanting to re-enter it again. But the shadow searched in vain . . . .

Only at April's end, when the fire chief had thrown himself in a fit of madness from a window of Dr. Zegota's sanatorium, dying on the spot, did his shadow stop visiting his house . . . .

Yet to this day legends circulate among people concerning the spirit of 'Fireproof,' which abandoning its body in sleep could not return to it, as it had been taken over by the elementals.

IN THE COMPARTMENT

The train shot through the landscape as quick as a flash.

Fields plunging into the darkness of evening, fallows bare and stark moved submissively behind, appearing like so many segments of a continuously folding fan. Taut telegraph wires went up, then went down, and once again unreeled with perfect, level straightness – stubborn, absurd, stiff lines . . . .

Godziemba was looking through the compartment window. His eyes, glued to the shiny rails, drank in their apparent movement; his hands, digging into the window sill, seemed to be helping the train push away the ground that was being passed. His heart rate was fast, as if wanting to increase the tempo of the ride, to double the momentum of the hollow-sounding wheels . . . .

A bird, inspired by the passage of the rushing locomotive, flew easily from the fetters of dreary existence and flashed by the lengthy coach walls, brushing their windows in its exhilarated flight and overtaking the engine to soar to the wide, vanishing horizon, to a faraway, mist-covered world! . . .

Godziemba was a train fanatic. This usually quiet and timid dreamer became unrecognizable the moment he mounted the steps of a coach. Gone was his unease and timidity, and his passive, musing eyes took on a sparkle of energy and strength. This notorious day-dreamer and sluggard was suddenly transformed into a dynamic, strong-willed person with a feeling of self-worth. And when the horn signal faded and the black coaches started toward their distant destinations, a boundless joy permeated his entire being, pouring warm and reviving currents into the farthest reaches of his soul, like the rays of the sun on summer days.

Something resided in the essence of a speeding train which galvanized Godziemba's weak nerves, stimulating strongly, though artificially, his faint life-force. A specific environment was created, a unique milieu of motion with its own laws, power and dangerous spirit. The motion of a locomotive was not just physically contagious; the momentum of an engine quickened his psychic pulse, it electrified his will – he became independent. 'Train neurosis' seemed to temporarily give this overly sensitive individual a forceful and positive energy. A moving train effected him like morphine injected into an addict's veins.

Finding himself inside the four walls of a compartment, Godziemba became instantly enlivened. This reclusive misanthrope initiated conversations and showered his fellow travellers with witty and impromptu anecdotes. An oaf – who aside from his remarkable transformation aboard a train was undistinguished in everything else – became a bold and incisive person. This shy individual changed unexpectedly into a blustering brawler, who could even be dangerous.

Quite a few times during a journey Godziemba had gone through some interesting adventures from which he emerged triumphant thanks to his pugnacious and unyielding attitude. A sarcastic witness to one such scene, who knew Godziemba well, advised him to settle all his affairs of honour in a train – and one travelling at full speed

'*Mon cher*, always duel in coaches; you'll fight like a lion. As God is my witness!'

But the artificial intensity of his life-force effected his health badly: he paid the price for almost every journey he made with an illness. After each temporary increase of psychological powers an even more violent reaction would follow, and he would descend into a state of even deeper prostration. Despite this, Godziemba liked riding trains immensely and repeatedly invented fictional travel goals just to drug himself with speed and motion.

So, yesterday evening, getting on the express at B., he really didn't know what he would do tonight at F., where in a few hours the train would deposit him. What did it matter to him, after all? For here he sits comfortably in a warm compartment, looking through the window at the landscape whisking by, and he is riding at 100 kilometres an hour . . . .

Meanwhile, outside it had darkened completely. A lamp near the ceiling, turned on by an unseen hand, vividly lit up the interior. Godziemba drew the curtain, turned his back to the window, and glanced at the compartment. Having been engrossed with the murky countryside, he hadn't noticed that at one of the stations two people had entered his compartment to occupy the empty seats opposite him.

Now in the lamp's yellow light he saw his fellow passengers. They were probably newly-weds. The man, tall, lean, with dark blonde hair and a clipped moustache, appeared to be in his thirties. From under his heavily-defined brows looked out bright, cheerful eyes. The sincere, somewhat long face was enhanced by a pleasant smile whenever he would turn to his companion.

The woman, also blonde but with a lighter hue, was small but well developed. Her luxuriant hair, twisted unpretentiously in two thick braids at the back of her head, framed a face which was delicate, fresh and attractive. The short grey dress, clasped simply with a leather belt, emphasized the alluring curves of her hips and firm, young breasts.

Both travellers were heavily covered with the dust and dirt of the roads; they were apparently returning from an outing. An aura of youth and health came from them – that refreshing vigour which mountain-climbing inspires in tourists. They were occupied in a lively conversation. It seemed they were sharing impressions of their excursion, for the first words Godziemba heard referred to some uncomfortable summit hostel.

'It's a pity we didn't take that woollen blanket with us; you know, the one with the red stripes,' said the young lady. 'It was a bit too cold.'

'Shame on you, Nuna,' scolded her companion with a smile. 'One shouldn't admit to being so weak. Do you have my cigarette case?'

Nuna plunged her hand into the travelling bag and withdrew the requested article.

'Here, but I think it's empty.'

'Let me see.'

He opened it. His face registered the disappointment of a fervent smoker.

'Too bad.'

Godziemba, who had managed several times to catch the glance of the vivacious blonde, took advantage of the opportunity and, removing his hat, politely offered his abundantly-filled cigarette case.

'Can I be of service?'

Returning his bow, the other man drew out a cigar.

'A thousand thanks. An impressive arsenal! Battery beside battery. You are more far-sighted than I, sir. Next time I'll supply myself better for the road.'

The preliminaries were successfully passed; a leisurely conversation commenced, flowing along smooth, wide channels.

The Rastawieckis were returning from the mountains after an eight-day excursion made partly on foot, partly on bicycles. Twice rain had drenched them in the ravines; once they had lost their way in some dead-end gully. Despite this, they ultimately overcame their difficulties, and the vacation had turned out splendidly. Now they were returning by train, quite tired but in excellent humour. They might have had one more week of fun among the ranges of the East Beskids if not for the engineer's surveying job. Anticipating an avalanche of work in the near future, Rastawiecki was just taking this short break. He was going back gladly, for he liked his work.

Godziemba listened only casually to these explanations, divided between the engineer and his wife; instead, he was taken up with Nuna's physical allurements.

One couldn't call her beautiful; she was just very pleasant and maddeningly enticing. Her plump, slightly stocky body exuded health and freshness, and aroused his libido with its seductive odours of wild herbs and thyme.

From the moment he saw her large blue eyes, he felt an irresistible attraction. This was odd, for she didn't fit his ideal. He preferred brunettes with slender waists and Roman profiles. Nuna belonged to the exact opposite type. Besides, Godziemba didn't get excited easily; he was by nature rather cold, and in sexual relations abstinent.

Yet all it took was a meeting of their eyes to kindle a secret fire of lust within him.

So he looked at her intensely; he followed her every movement, her every change of position.

Had she noticed anything? Once he caught an embarrassed glance thrown furtively from under her silky eyebrows – and he also thought he had detected on her luscious cherry lips a little smile full of pride and coquetry meant for him.

This stimulated Godziemba. He became daring. During the conversation he slowly moved away from the window and shifted imperceptibly closer to her knees. He felt them opposite his and their pleasant warmth radiating through the grey, woollen dress.

Then, when the coach gave a slight tilt at a turn, their knees met. For a few seconds he drank in the sweetness of the touch. He pressed harder, nestled there, and, with inexpressible joy, felt he was being similarly answered. Was this an accident?

No. Nuna didn't withdraw her legs; on the contrary, she crossed one over the other in such a manner that her slightly raised thigh hid Godziemba's slightly too persistent knee from her husband. In this manner, they journeyed for an exquisitely long time . . . .

Godziemba was in an excellent mood. He told jokes and even ribald stories that just managed to be respectable. The engineer's wife continually burst out with ripples of silvery laughter, revealing in sparkling profusion, a little predatorily, her even, glazed teeth. The movement of her rounded hips, shaking with her quivering laughter, was soft, feline, almost lascivious.

Godziemba's cheeks became flushed, his eyes sparkled

with passion and intoxication. An overpowering aura of lust exuded from him, bewitching the engineer's wife.

Rastawiecki divided his gaiety among them. Some peculiar blindness threw an ever thicker curtain over the duplicitous behavior of his companion, some strange indulgence made him ignore his wife's deportment. Maybe he never had a reason to be suspicious of Nuna's flightiness, and that's why he acted thus? Maybe he didn't yet know the sex demon, suppressed under superficial domesticity, and had never been aware of its corrupting influence and deceitfulness? A fatal spell enfolded these three people in its domain and drove them toward frenzy and abandonment – one saw it in the spasmodic movements of Nuna's body, the blood-shot eyes of her admirer, the sardonic grimace of the husband's lips.

'Ha, ha, ha!' laughed Godziemba.

'Hi, hi, hi!' seconded the woman.

'He, he, he!' responded the engineer.

And the train rushed breathlessly along; it darted up hills, slid down valleys; it ripped up the landscape with its powerful chest. Rails rattled, wheels rumbled . . . .

Around one o'clock Nuna began to complain of a headache; the lamp's bright light bothered her. The obliging Godziemba let down the shade over it. From then on, they rode in semi-darkness.

The mood for conversation slowly died out. The words fell infrequently, interrupted by the yawning of the engineer's wife; the lady was apparently sleepy. She tilted her head backward, leaning it against her husband's shoulder. But the legs that were carelessly stretched out toward the opposite seat didn't lose contact with her neighbour's; on the contrary, now in the darkened atmosphere they were considerably more unrestrained. Godziemba felt them continually, as their sweet weight exerted an inert pressure on his shinbone.

Rastawiecki, wearied by travel, hung his head on his chest. Sinking between the plush cushions, he fell asleep. Shortly, in the quiet of the compartment, one could hear his even, calm breathing. Silence prevailed . . . .

Godziemba was not asleep. Stimulated erotically, burning like iron in a fire, he had merely closed his eyelids in pretence. Through his body coursed hot streams of strongly pulsating blood; a delicious lethargy unravelled the elasticity of his limbs; lust took control of his mind.

He delicately placed his hand on Nuna's leg and felt her firm flesh with his fingers. A sweet giddiness misted his eyes. He moved his hand higher, imagining the silky touch of her body . . . .

Suddenly her hips undulated with a shiver of pleasure; she stretched out her hand and plunged it into his hair. The silent caress lasted but a moment . . . .

He raised his head and met the moist glance of her passionate eyes. With her finger she indicated the second half of the compartment, even darker than where they were. He understood. He got up, slid past the sleeping engineer, and, tiptoeing, went to the other half of the compartment. Here, covered by dense obscurity and a partition that reached his chest, he sat down in excited anticipation.

But the rustling which had occurred despite all caution woke up Rastawiecki. He rubbed his eyes and glanced around. Nuna, nestling down momentarily in the corner of the compartment, pretended to be dozing. The place opposite her was empty.

The engineer yawned slowly and straightened up.

'Quiet, Mieciek!' she reprimanded him with a sleepy pout. 'It's late.'

'Sorry. Where is that – satyr?'

'What satyr?'

'I dreamt of a satyr with the face of that gentleman who was sitting opposite us.'

'He probably got off somewhere. Now you have the space to stretch out. Get comfortable and go to sleep. I'm tired.'

'Good advice.'

He yawned again, stretched himself out on the oilcloth cushions, and placed an overcoat under his head.

'Good-night, Nuna.'

'Good-night.'

Silence fell.

With bated breath, Godziemba had been crouching behind the partition during this brief scene, waiting for the dangerous moment to pass. From his dark corner, he only saw the engineer's empty, still boots projecting beyond the edge of the bench, and, on the opposite seat, Nuna's grey silhouette. Mrs. Rastawiecki remained in the same position as her husband had found her after his awakening. But her open eyes glowed in the semi-darkness hungrily, wildly, provocatively. Thus passed fifteen minutes of travelling.

Suddenly, against the background of the rattling of the coach, sharp snoring sounds came from the engineer's open mouth. Rastawiecki was soundly asleep. Then, nimble like a cat, his wife got off the cushions and found herself in Godziemba's arms. With a silent but powerful kiss they connected their craving lips and became entangled in a long, hungry embrace. Her young, robust breasts pressed burningly against him, and she gave him the fragrant conch of her body . . . .

Godziemba took her. He took her like a flame in the swelter of a conflagration that destroys and consumes and burns; he took her like a gale in unbridled, unrestrained frenzy, a savage wind of the steppe. Dormant lust exploded with a red cry and tore at the bit. Pleasure, bridled at first by fear and the affectation of prudence, finally broke out triumphantly in a rich scarlet wave.

Nuna writhed in passion, she bucked with spasms of boundless love and pain. Her body, bathed in mountain streams, swarthy from the winds of mountain pastures, smelled of herbs thick, raw and giddy. Her young vaulted hips, soft at the buttocks, were opening up like private tufts of a rose, and they drank and sucked in love's tribute. Freed from its binding clips, her flaxen hair fell smoothly over her shoulders and enclosed him. Sobs shook her chest, her parched lips threw out words and entreaties . . . .

Suddenly Godziemba felt a tangible pain at the back of

his head, and almost simultaneously he heard Nuna's distressful cry. Half-conscious, he turned around and at the same time received a strong blow on his cheek. Blood rushed to his head, fury twisted his lips. Like lightning he countered the next intended punch as his fist smashed his opponent between the eyes. Rastawiecki reeled, but didn't fall down. A fierce fight commenced in the semi-darkness.

The engineer was a tall, strong man, yet the frenzy of victory immediately tilted toward Godziemba. In this individual, by all appearances slender and weak, some feverish, pronounced strength had been awakened. An evil, demonic strength raised his frail arms, inflicted blows, neutralized the attack. Wild, blood-shot eyes predatorily watched the enemy's movements, they read his thoughts, anticipated his actions.

The two men struggled in the quiet of a night disrupted by the rumble of the train, the noise of their feet, and the quick breathing of overworked lungs. They struggled in silence like two boars fighting over a female, who was cuddled in a corner of the compartment.

Because of the tight confines, the fight was restricted to an extremely narrow area between the seats, moving from one part of the compartment to the other. Gradually the opponents tired each other out. Big drops of sweat flowed down from exhausted foreheads; hands, weak from punching, were lifted up ever more heavily. Already Godziemba had stumbled onto the cushions from a well-measured push; but in the next second he was up. Gathering his remaining strength, he used his knee to thrust away his opponent; then with enraged momentum he threw him to the opposite corner of the compartment. The engineer staggered like a drunk, the weight of his body broke open the door. Before he got a chance to stand up, Godziemba was shoving him toward the platform. Here was played out the final short and relentless act of the battle.

The engineer defended himself weakly, parrying with difficulty his opponent's frenzied fury. Blood was running down his forehead, lips, nose – and pouring over his eyes.

Suddenly Godziemba rammed him with the full weight of his body. Rastawiecki lost his balance, reeled, and fell under the wheels of the train. His hoarse scream drowned out the groan of the rails and the rumble of the coaches . . . .

The victor breathed freely. He drew into his exhausted chest the cool night air, rubbed the sweat from his forehead, and straightened his crumpled clothes. The wind of the rushing train streamed through his hair and cooled his hot blood. He lit up a cigarette. He felt somehow refreshed, happy.

He calmly opened the door that had slammed shut during the fight, and with a sure step returned to the compartment. As he entered, warm, serpentine arms embraced him. In her eyes glowed the question:

'Where is he? Where is my husband?'

'He will never return,' he answered indifferently.

She cuddled against him.

'You will protect me from the world. My beloved!'

He embraced her strongly.

'I don't know what is happening to me,' she whispered, leaning against his chest. 'I feel such a sweet giddiness in my head. We've committed a great sin, but I'm not afraid beside you, my strength. Poor Mieciek! . . . . You know it's terrible, but I'm not sorry for him. Why, that's horrible! He's my husband!'

She drew back suddenly, but looking into his eyes, intoxicated with the fire of love, she forgot everything. They started to devise plans for the future. Godziemba was a rich man and of independent means – no occupation tied him down, he could leave the country at any time and take up residence anywhere in the world . . . . So, they will get off at the nearest station, where the rail lines cross, and go south. The connection will be excellent – at daybreak the express to Trieste departs. He'll buy the tickets immediately, and in twelve hours they'll reach the port. From there, a ship will take them to a land of oranges where a May sun sweetens trees, where the ocean's deep-blue chest washes golden sand, and flowers adorn pagan temples.

He spoke in a calm voice, sure of his manly aims, indifferent toward the judgement of people. Full of energy, ready to contend with the world, he lifted her collapsing figure.

Nuna, who had been listening intently to the sound of his words, appeared to be dreaming some strange, singular fairy tale, some golden, wonderful story . . . .

The engine's loud whistle announced the station. Godziemba trembled.

'It's time. Let's get our things together.'

She got up and took down her travel coat from the overhanging net. He helped her dress.

Streaks of the station's lamplights shone through their window. A protracted shudder once again shook Godziemba.

The train stopped. They left the compartment and descended to the station platform. They were swept up and absorbed by the multitude, by the tumult of voices and lights.

Suddenly, Nuna, leaning on his arm, weighed heavily on him like fate. In the twinkling of an eye, somewhere from the corner of his soul, dread crept in, an insane dread, and it made his hair stand on end. A feverishly drawn mouth cried out the danger. Horrible, base fear bared its sharp claws . . . .

He was just a murderer and a despicable coward.

In the midst of the greatest throng, he freed his arm from Nuna's embrace, stepped away from her without being noticed, and made his way through some dark corridor to the outside of the station. A maddened flight ensued along the back-streets of an unknown city . . . .

SATURNIN SEKTOR

Someone has sought me out! Someone has tracked me down! I live so isolated, so outside the commotion of the world – yet someone is spying on me. And it is precisely because of Duration that this fact has revealed itself, a fact so tied-up with my 'insane,' as sensible people have stated, person. Most interesting!

On July 20th of the so-called 'current year' (I'm speaking here in their style), a significant article titled 'The Evolution of Time' appeared in one of the leading newspapers. The author signed it with the initials S.S. The treatise was written incisively, forcefully and with confidence, as befits someone who vigorously holds onto 'life' and immerses himself up to the neck in 'reality.' It has no value for me. The viewpoint is, of course, 'realistic.' A panegyric praising human intellect and its creations.

But the article concerns me for other reasons. It is clearly directed against me and my convictions about so-called 'time.' The unknown author defends time, while endeavouring to shatter my charges, which he appears to know quite well. But how? At the moment, this is a mystery.

I haven't exchanged even one word with anyone on the topic of time and its non-existence; I have not delivered one lecture; I have not put out the thinnest book or pamphlet. No one in the world has read my treatise 'On the False Conception and Fictitiousness of Time.' No one knows, no one can know, of the existence of such a work. Not one of my few acquaintances, who have eagerly withdrawn from me since my return from the asylum, even suspects that I ever occupied myself in any way with this problem. The fruit of many years of reflection and study rests quietly inside a black oilcloth portfolio here in my desk, in a secret hiding place on the right, to which no one has access without my knowledge. Absolutely no one. Yet this person definitely knows the content of the manuscript – and he knows it by heart, inside and out. And he's attempting to shatter my 'opinion,' as he terms it. The idiot! – my certainty! Even the arrangement of thoughts is the same, even the counter-arguments are drawn from the same sources. My adversary seizes my expressions, my definitions; he alters to his style values and concepts discovered by me; he shamelessly distorts the laborious investigations of my entire life for his own use. This is peculiar, most, most peculiar!

Somehow he became aware of me. He read my thoughts from a distance and answered them like an adversary. Some mysterious connection must exist between us then, some spiritual link that makes something like this possible.

But I do not wish this upon myself at all. I do not like to be spied on, even if unconsciously, even if from afar. This person is a great inconvenience, and I will try to remove him at all cost.

At the moment I do not know anything about him. I was already at the editorial office of the newspaper which printed the article, and I demanded to know the name of the author. They replied that they did not know. The manuscript had arrived by mail from someone in the locality, but without a signature – just the initials S.S. The article was interesting, it touched on a topical subject, treated it in an excellent and learned fashion, and could not be faulted. Therefore, it was printed.

Maybe this is true, or maybe that secretive editorial office is lying. But he will not escape me! I will find him sooner or later – if not in the usual manner, then in my own way. I have behind me their help: mysterious, unseen by the eyes of the 'healthy.' They visit me almost every day and carry on long, private talks. Their access to me was made easier by my 'insanity' . . . .

How stupid are 'healthy,' 'normal' people! How I sincerely feel sorry for them! These morons do not know the wonderful other half of existence. They merely hold onto 'reality' with both hands, and they don't see anything else beyond it. They live their entire lives this way until 'death' finally bars them from the other side.

I belong to a chosen few who are freely allowed to cross from one side to the other. Thanks to my 'insanity' I stand on the border between two worlds. Maybe it is precisely because of this that I am liberated from the superstitions and 'reasonings' of the mind. The mind's prejudices are alien to me and put me under no obligation. The idea of time does not exist for me.

Yet I am still somewhat hampered. I cannot free myself from that strong, commanding voice which speaks to me, or from that mysterious power which pushes aside objects, contemptuous of their size; I am still wearied by endless, monotonous roads that lead nowhere. That is why I am not a perfect spirit, only an 'insane person,' someone who arouses in normal people pity, contempt or fear. But I do not complain. Even like this, I am better off than those of healthy mind.

Distant, misty lands unfold before me, enchanting precipices, unknown worlds with gloomy depths. I am visited by the dead, by processions of strange creatures and capricious elemental beings. One appears, the other leaves — ethereal, beautiful, dangerous . . . .

*   *   *

One of the waves of Duration has cast on the threshold of my home a new figure — as yet I do not know if he is 'real' or from that other side.

He comes in the evening; it is unknown how or from where. He stands close by and stares at me for hours without saying a word.

He has the look of antiquity about him. His face is Roman, shaved, without a trace of growth — a face swarthy, almost grey. His age is indeterminate: sometimes he looks fifty years old, sometimes a hundred or more; his features change most oddly. Yet I feel that he must be a very old man.

In his right hand he holds a scythe, in his left, an hourglass that he raises to the light from time to time, examining the position of the sand.

In the beginning he was stubbornly silent and did not answer any of my questions. Only after his tenth visit did he allow himself to be drawn into a conversation. From the start it went ploddingly and hard, for my guest is evidently taciturn and does not possess the appropriate verbal skills.

'Put aside that scythe,' I urged him by way of greeting. 'You have carried it needlessly for so many years. Today it doesn't make the right impression – it has become a lifeless reminder of the past.'

My visitor's face twisted itself into a malicious grimace. For the first time a voice issued forth from his lips, a voice wooden, without resonance:

'You think so? I think otherwise. I am Tempus.'

'So I guessed. Greetings, Saturn! To what do I owe the pleasure of this visit?'

'You have been looking for me for some time. So here I am.'

'You . . . do not exist. You are an illusion.'

'I have materialized, as you can see. For too long people have spoken of me – therefore I've assumed this body. I have been lured out of non-existence.'

'Maybe. But this get-up? It's a little old-fashioned. You're out of date, my dear sir.'

'No matter. A typical rigidity of a thrombotic allegory. Besides, mankind can clothe me in new garments. It's even high time that they did. I am already sick of these rags. They make me look like an anachronism.'

He contemptuously tugged at the flaps of the heavily-frayed toga.

'So you see, my friend, I was right.'

'In part, yes, as far as the attire is concerned. But you apparently do not acknowledge my existence at all.'

'Naturally. You are a fiction of the mind. If I concern myself with the question of your costume, then I act only from the point of view of the "healthy." You have apparently passed through an evolution, eh? So, at least, I've read.'

Saturn's mask brightened up in a triumphant smile:

'Ah! So you read the article? Wasn't it beautifully written? Yes, yes, I have developed. I am already not conceived of today as I once was in the ancient world. I've become a changed value, independent, which knowledge attempts to introduce everywhere. I have been divided into minutes, seconds; I influence every moment. I've become precise, refined . . . .'

'Oh, certainly! You've become devilishly lean! To the dimensions of the hands of a clock. You've desecrated the sacred mystery of Duration, you've marred the wonderful fluidity of the waves – you despoiler of life!' Crying this out, I sprang up from my seat.

My visitor was already at the threshold.

'I am stronger than you,' I heard his measured voice say, calm like the movement of a pendulum. 'For behind me is reality and people who are healthy and practical. And I am indispensable. Farewell! You will find me in the city in a somewhat more modern form.'

I wanted to forcibly stop him, but he slipped away and disappeared beyond the door . . . .

In the sky, the sunset was dying out. I sat alone in an empty room . . . .

★　　　★　　　★

Since then, Tempus did not show up at my home anymore. Accomplishing some mission, he withdrew, never to return. But his words gave me no rest and rang in my ears with the intrusive refrain:

'You will find me in the city.'

What did this mean? Was it a call to battle? Meanwhile, articles dealing with time were appearing in the newspapers, their pointed arguments apparently directed against me. All were signed with the mysterious initials S.S. They dwelled on the profoundness of the notion of time, and endlessly underlined time's efficiency and its usefulness in regulating life. In a word, they were paeans of worship for my visitor.

Irritated by these sallies, I collected and studied them, while strengthening my treatise with new proofs and arguments. I was preparing myself, while I waited for my opponent to run out of ideas; at that point, I would publish my response.

Simultaneously, I was searching for my antagonist. I roamed about the city until the late evening hours, peeking into cafés, striking up conversations with acquaintances, drawing people into discourses on the subject of time. In this way I became introduced to several professors, to learned philosophers, and to some dozen or so various eccentrics and characters. But I always left dissatisfied from the debates with these gentlemen. Admittedly, the problem seemed to absorb them on a rather high level, but even so, one didn't sense the same ardour which emerged from the newspaper columns. These were not opponents; not one person took the issue so personally, with so much passion and belief, as that unknown one.

Gradually I'm becoming convinced that I've fallen on a false trail, that the sphere in which one should look for him lies a little 'lower' . . . .

*   *   *

It seems that I'm finally on the right track. As of yesterday evening . . . .

After roaming about all day, I am returning home. I'm going by the old section of the city that stretches up from the river in a system of rough little streets. I cut across them, struggling up the incline. Above me, patches of evening sky, marred by chimney smoke, look over filthy tenements. Pale, consumptive faces and the unkempt heads of old hags lean out of windows; the stagnant, bleary eyes of the aged stare at me . . . .

Stumbling over the holes and bumps in the pavement, I turn into a narrow street and glance down to its end. There, far in the distance, the river bleeds under the agony of the sunset, its water glittering with melancholic waves.

127

Somewhere overhead, from some crumbling ruin, a flock of crows takes flight and, forming a heavily patterned arch, disappears beyond the roofs of the buildings. I lower my gaze and my weary eyes survey forlorn windows. My glance stops on some sign – on the black letters of someone's name set against a faded green background. I look blankly, unable to combine the words. Suddenly I formulate them: Saturnin Sektor, Watchmaker.

Most certainly! It is he! I've found him at last!

A great peace fills my soul, and slowly I start to return home . . . .

A strange thing! I live close by.

It even seems that here, next door – only I've come up to my home from a different direction than I usually take, a direction I haven't ever taken until now. After thirty years of residence in the city! Remarkable! And yet it happens at times that a person returns home one way for many years, walking continually the same route day after day, until finding himself on a different path at a certain moment, he discovers with amazement that it also leads to his home – the amazement of a person who has been dreaming for many long years, until one day he awakens on an unknown road leading to his own interior . . . .

So this is the name of my opponent, and he is a watchmaker. Of course it is he, only he and no one else. I only wonder why I haven't come upon him before. The name is known to me from somewhere; it is so familiar. I cannot, admittedly, recall from where – but this doesn't in any way affect my deep, firm conviction that I know this person. I realized immediately that he is my oppressor, the mysterious stranger whom I've been seeking for so long.

The very name is significant! It says so much about itself! Let us first analyse his forename. Saturnin! Doesn't it strike a clear connection with Saturn-Time? Doesn't this name immediately cast a vision of the old man with the scythe and hourglass? So the name is obviously symbolic.

And the surname Sektor – it's odd, isn't it? No, it's exquisitely chosen! Sektor – in actuality Sector – that's something cut up, shredded into sections, segments, divisions. How much hidden self-irony is in this nickname! But does it not perfectly suit his work? Indeed, he has deformed the wonder of Duration into mathematical abstractions; he has chopped up the flowing, undivided wave of life into a multitude of dead divisions. Sektor – a symbol of years, months, days, minutes, seconds. He has enclosed in two words the essence of his untruthful, negative activity. A dangerous person – a symbol! As long as he lives, mankind will not shake off the fallacy of time and follow me. That's why one should erase this name from the memory of the living and replace it with mine. Mine?! . . . What a remarkable thought! My name! . . . My name . . . . What is my name? . . . I cannot remember . . . . This is funny, this is very funny! This is humiliating! . . . I've forgotten, completely forgotten my name. I am anonymous – yes – anonymous – as a wave in the ocean – a wave that is eternally flowing into another wave – and another wave – and another . . . .

*　　　　*　　　　*

After a long, sleepless night, I am on my way to meet him. Rotting, squeaky stairs, their boards full of holes, lead me on. I open the door and enter.

The snug old room murmurs with the voices of clocks. And there are an endless number of them: black ebonies creeping along the walls like large scarabaei, round antiques on ivory columns, French baroques under glass bells, playful, loudly ticking alarms. In a niche covered with green fabric whisper the half-century prayers of small 'pocket-watches,' golden, marvellously enamelled 'turnips,' silver, inlaid 'repeaters,' expensive miniatures adorned in ruby and emerald.

In the middle of the room is a small table with a watchmaker's tools: a chisel, pincers, a group of screws, springs as thin as hairs, ringlets, metal plates. On a patch of green woollen cloth lie a pair of damaged watchcases, several newly-extracted diamonds . . . .

On a stool, leaning over some clock, he sits – the master of time. Through the dust whirling in the shaft of sunlight falling through the window, I can make out his face. It is somehow well known to me. I've seen it somewhere, where – I can't remember. Maybe in a mirror. A grey, old head with ginger side-whiskers and sharp, vulture-like features.

He raises his bright, piercing eyes, and he smiles at me. A strange, strange smile.

'I would like to have a watch repaired.'

'You are lying, my friend – you haven't used a watch for ten years. Why these subterfuges?'

His voice pierces me to the core; I've heard it somewhere, and I know it well – the voice is very familiar.

'I know why you have come. I've been waiting for you for a long time.'

Now, I smile.

'If so, then the matter is greatly simplified.'

'Naturally. Before you fulfil your purpose – sit down. We'll have a talk. Why, we have plenty of time.'

'Of course. I'm in no hurry.'

I sit down and listen intently to the conversation of the clocks. They run uniformly to the minute, to the second.

'You've regulated time perfectly here,' I remark casually.

Sektor is silent, his eyes fixed on me.

I take up the thread of the conversation with difficulty. 'So you are prepared for everything?'

'Yes. I will not defend myself.'

'Why? You have a right to, as does every person.'

'It would be pointless. I feel that shortly your era will arrive, no matter what. As an ideal symbol of an age about to pass, I yield before inevitability. An unpicked fruit eventually falls off a tree by itself.'

'Therefore you acknowledge me?'

'No. This is different. Even you will one day have to yield to a new symbol. Let us not forget about the relativity of ideas. Everything depends on one's point of view.'

'Exactly. Even so, where do you get that certainty that runs through your articles?'

'It springs from a deep conviction about the usefulness of what I proclaim.'

'Ah, that's true. You belong to that generation whose ideal is practical reality.'

'Yes, yes. You, on the other hand, reach beyond it; at least it appears so to you. And you fall into a hazy *mare tenebrarum*. For people of flesh and blood this is not enough; they need reality and everything that confirms it.'

'You are mistaken. I only wish the deepening of life. Life flows in wide, dense waves, in occurrences tied together so compactly that their division into years, months, days, hours, minutes and seconds is absurd. Your notion of time is simply a fanciful concoction drawn from imaginary theories.'

'Isn't time a beautiful idea? Have you read *The Time Machine* by that famous English author?'

'Certainly. In fact, I had it on my mind. It is the best example as to where the imagination can lead. The very idea of a "time machine," doesn't it offend life's virginity with its abundance of constant surprises? These are the results of the vivisection you perform on it. This is an example of how one mechanizes life.'

'A fabulous story. The quintessence of the mind and its majestic might.'

'You are the fool, my dear sir. Rest assured – no one will ever travel into the past or the future in a machine.'

'We will never understand each other. A peculiar circumstance! Even though our beings are so intertwined.'

At that moment a terrible chill ran through my body. The watchmaker's words came to me as if from my own self.

'Hmm, indeed. At times I feel this too.'

'If it weren't for the fact,' continued the old man in a crestfallen voice, 'that your thoughts are like new seedlings planted in a barren field, if I didn't have a presentiment of their blossoming in the immediate future . . . .'

'Then what?'

'I would kill you,' he coldly replied. 'With this instrument.'

He extracted from a plush box of wonderful workmanship an ivory-handled dagger.

I smiled triumphantly:

'Meanwhile the roles are reversed.'

The old man lowered his head in resignation:

'Because you've overcome me in yourself . . . . Now go. I still want to write my last will. Come back in the evening. Take this as a memento.'

He handed me the dagger.

I mechanically took the glittering, cool steel, and without a word of farewell, I left. As I walked down the stairs, I heard a cackling sound coming from the workshop. The old man was laughing . . . .

—   —   —

The evening papers of W. gave the following information in their columns:

Murder or Suicide?

A mysterious incident occurred last night at 10 Water Street. This morning Rozalia Witkowska, a widow of a private official, discovered the dead body of a watchmaker, Saturnin Sektor, when she entered his workshop. The body, seated by a window, was covered with blood. An antique dagger of delicate workmanship was buried in the victim's chest.

At Mrs. Witkowska's screams the neighbours rushed in, then the police. The medical examiner, Dr. Obminski, confirmed the death, which most probably occurred during the night as a result of blood loss. There were no signs of robbery. Instead, on a table near the body, Policeman Tulejko found the dead man's will and a sheet of paper on which the watchmaker had apparently jotted down the following words:

'Do not look for any assailants. I die by my own hand.'

The incident exhibits many mysterious and unclear features. Already various rumours are circulating about the deceased. Apparently Sektor spent a few years in an asylum, from which he was only recently released. The director of the institution, a Dr. Tumin, was summoned as a witness in this puzzling matter and stated that the watchmaker had long been suffering from periodic bouts of madness, which grew stronger at every recurrence. This statement is supported by the testimony of Sektor's neighbours and co-tenants in the apartment house. He had the reputation of being insane. None the less, at periods of *lucida intervalla* he devoted himself to his professional activities, fulfilling a watchmaker's function excellently. His acquaintances even considered him a brilliant watchmaker.

An interesting light is thrown on the matter by the deceased's will. Sektor bequeaths all of his substantial fortune for the endowment of an educational fund, with the special stipulation that it be used exclusively by those researching the problem of space and time, as well as any related issues.

Simultaneously with the mysterious incident at Water Street, a couple of sensational facts were reported to police headquarters and the municipal clerk. Strange placards and announcements have been found on the walls of the city in the form of obituary notices, bearing the following message:

The Death Of Time

On the night of November 29th of the current year, Tempus Saturn died, never to return, yielding his place to perpetual Duration.

133

The second, equally puzzling aspect is that all the tower clocks of our town have stopped for no apparent reason. The hands halted last night at eleven.

A general agitation and some peculiar, superstitious fear reign in the town. Frightened crowds gather in the public squares; voices are heard connecting strange manifestations with the death of the watchmaker.

THE GLANCE

It had begun then – four years ago, on that August afternoon when Jadwiga left his house for what proved to be the last time. That day she was somehow different. She was quite nervous, as if expecting something. And she held onto him more passionately than ever before.

Then, suddenly, she quickly got dressed, threw over her head her distinctive Venetian scarf, and, kissing him forcefully on the lips, departed. One more time the hem of her dress and the slender outline of her shoe whisked by the threshold, and everything ended forever . . . .

An hour later she perished under the wheels of a train. Odonicz never found out if her death was accidental or if Jadwiga had thrown herself under the speeding engine. She was, after all, an unpredictable person, that swarthy, dark-eyed woman.

But this was not the issue. Truly, it was not. The pain, the despair, the inconsolable grief – all of this was quite natural and understandable. Therefore, this was not the issue.

What struck one was something completely different – something so ridiculously trivial, something so secondary . . . . Jadwiga, upon leaving him that time, had left the door open.

He remembered that he had stumbled while escorting her through the room, and that, irritated, he had bent down to straighten out a folded corner of the carpet. When he raised his eyes a moment later, Jadwiga was no longer there. She had departed, leaving the door open.

Why hadn't she closed it? She was usually such a conscientious woman, at times meticulously so . . . .

He remembered that unpleasant, that most unpleasant impression which the open door had made on him, fluttering its black, smoothly lacquered leaf like a mourning banner in the wind. He was annoyed by its restless movement, which intermittently hid before his eyes a portion of the square in front of his house, to then reveal it in the afternoon sunlight. As he stood there, it suddenly crossed his mind that Jadwiga had left him forever, leaving behind some complex problem to be unravelled whose outward expression was the open door.

Seized by this ominous premonition, he had sprung to the swinging door and looked to his right, in the direction she would have probably taken. There was no trace of her. Before him, spreading out to the railroad embankment in the far horizon, was a golden, empty square, scorching-hot from the summer's heat. Nothing but that golden, sun-intoxicated plain . . . . Afterwards came a long, dull ache lasting several months and a silent, heart-wrenching despair born of loss . . . . Then everything passed – somehow it went away, withdrawing to a corner somewhere . . . .

And then came this. Stealthily, imperceptibly, from neither here nor there, as if by mere chance. The problem of the open door . . . . Ha! ha! ha! The problem! A mockery, indeed! The problem of the open door. It's difficult to believe. Yes, it is. And yet, and yet . . . .

For entire nights this stubborn nightmare revolved in his mind; he saw the door during the day whenever he momentarily closed his eyes; it appeared in the midst of bright, sober reality – illusive, distant, yet seemingly real.

But now it wasn't tossed about by the wind, as it had been in that fatal hour. Now it moved slowly, very slowly, away from the fictitious doorframe – as if someone on the outside, the side unseen by his eye, was holding the door-knob and carefully opening the door to a certain angle . . . .

It was precisely this carefulness, this very cautious movement, which chilled him to the bone. One dreaded the angle becoming too great, the door opening too wide. It seemed the door was playing around with him, not wanting to show what was hiding beyond it. Only the edge of the mystery was revealed to him. He was given the knowledge that there, on the other side, beyond the door, a mystery existed, but any greater details were jealously concealed.

Odonicz fought against this frustrating suggestion with all his might. A thousand times a day he convinced himself that beyond his front door there wasn't anything alarming, that beyond all his doors nothing was lurking. He constantly tore himself away from his work, and with a quick, predatory step, the step of a stalking panther, he would spring to each door, and, nearly ripping off the lock, open each one and glance into the space beyond. Always, of course, with the same result: not once did he find anything suspicious. Before his eyes, which sought out with terrified curiosity any trace of mystery, there unfolded, just as in the good old days, only an empty, barren square, only the banal fragment of a corridor or the quiet and still interior of the adjoining bedroom or bathroom.

Then he would return to his desk somewhat pacified, only to succumb again to his obsessive thoughts several minutes later .... Finally, he consulted a highly eminent neurologist and began treatment. He went to the seaside several times, he took cold baths, he started going to parties.

After a while it seemed everything had passed. The stubborn picture of the open door gradually faded — and finally vanished.

And Odonicz would have been completely satisfied with himself if not for certain manifestations which showed up a couple of months later.

And they came suddenly, unexpectedly, in a public place, on the street ....

He was close to the end of Swietojanski Street, nearing the point where it intersects with Polna, when at that corner, almost near the edge of the last tenement, panic seized him. It came from some nook and grabbed him by the throat with its iron claws.

'You won't go further, my dear sir! Not one step further!'

Odonicz had originally intended to turn directly onto Polna Street at the point where the tenement ended, when he felt this resistance. He didn't know why, but suddenly it seemed that the angle of the intersection was too sharp for his nerves. Quite simply, an overwhelming anxiety arose within him that there – 'beyond the bend,' 'around the corner' – one could meet with 'a surprise.'

The corner building, which one had to go around at an almost perfect right angle to turn onto Polna Street, shielded him for the time being from that unpleasant circumstance, hiding with its several-storied front a view of the other side. But eventually the wall would have to end, suddenly revealing, terrifyingly so, what was to the left of the corner. That suddenness, that instant crossing from one street to another as yet almost completely hidden from his eyes, seized him with boundless alarm. Odonicz didn't dare meet 'the unknown.' Therefore, he took the path of compromise, and closing his eyes before the turn, with his hand resting against the wall so as not to fall, he slowly swerved onto the new street.

In this manner, sliding his fingers along the surface of the wall, he advanced a few steps. When his fingers brushed by the arris of the building, he sensed that the turn had been successfully passed and that he had entered the zone of the next street. Even so, he didn't dare open his eyes, and he went down Polna Street feeling the walls of its buildings with his hand.

Only after several minutes, when he had already attained, as it were, the right of citizenship in the new zone, when he finally felt that his presence was known, did he get the courage to open his eyes. Looking ahead, he ascertained with relief that there was nothing suspicious before him. Everything was as ordinary and normal as on any urban street: carriages rushed by, motor-coaches flew like lightning, people were passing each other. Odonicz noticed, however, some empty-headed lout several steps away, who, hands thrust in his pockets, a cigarette dangling from his ugly mouth, was gazing at him quite openly and smiling maliciously.

Odonicz suddenly became seized with rage and shame. Flushed with emotion, he went up to the impertinent man, and asked harshly:

'Why are you gaping at me with your vacant eyes, you clown?'

'Ha, ha, ha,' let out the rascal casually, not removing the cigarette from his lips. 'At first I thought you were blind – but now I think you're only playing blindman's buff with yourself. Can you believe it! What an imagination!' And taking no more heed of Odonicz's enraged response, he crossed over to the other side of the street, whistling some arietta.

Thus, a new problem arose on the horizon: 'turning a corner.'

From then on Odonicz lost his self-confidence and relinquished his freedom of movement in public places. Unable to go from one street to the next without feeling an unknown anxiety, he adopted methods of circumventing turns by using wide circles. This was, admittedly, highly inconvenient, for he had to go greatly out of his way, but in this manner he avoided sudden turns, softening considerably the angle at which streets broke off. Now he didn't have to close his eyes at corner tenements anymore.

Any surprises which could eventually hide around the corner, now had enough time to mask themselves. That indefinite, heterogenous and bizarrely unfamiliar 'something,' whose existence on the other side of the turn he felt deeply, could now – not caught unawares by his sudden appearance – hide with relative ease for a while, or, speaking in Odonicz's expressive style, 'dive under the surface.' For by then he didn't doubt at all that there was something around the corner, something fundamentally different.

In any case, at least during this period, Odonicz did not wish a meeting with that 'something' face to face; on the contrary, he desired to step out of its way and also facilitate its own concealment. The terrible fright which possessed him at the very thought that some revelations could occur, some undesirable manifestations and surprises, merely strengthened his conviction that the danger was indeed real.

The opinion of people in this matter didn't concern him

at all. He felt that everyone should deal with this unknown presence by themselves – that is, if anyone besides himself was caught up in the same situation.

Odonicz clearly realized that perhaps he was the only person in the world to have noticed all of this. He even supposed that the majority of his dear fellow creatures would burst out in coarse laughter right in his face if he were bold enough to reveal his anxieties to them. That's why he was stubbornly silent, struggling alone with 'the unknown.'

Only after some time did he understand that the source of his particular phobia was a fear of mystery, that masked presence which has existed for ages and which walks, unseen and unsuspected, among people. But Odonicz, fearful and craving life, did not wish to confront it. That's why he shunned any sort of meeting and facilitated a mutual avoidance . . . .

Since the time of that inner resistance that had so unexpectedly come upon him at the corner of Polna Street, he developed a fundamental aversion for all walls and partitions – and also for temporary 'covers' that could offer concealment. He felt that all so-called 'screens' were a fatal, even unethical contrivance, for they made the dangerous game of hide-and-seek easier, besides frequently awakening suspicion and anxiety where there might be no trace of strangeness. Why hide things which do not merit concealment? Why unnecessarily arouse suspicion, as if something was there that needed concealing? And if that 'something' really existed – why offer it a means of playing hide-and-seek?

Odonicz became a strong advocate of distant, clear perspectives, wide squares, vast open spaces stretching far, far away, as far as the eye could see. On the other hand, he couldn't stand the ambiguity of alleys, insidiously hiding within the shadows of arcades, the hypocrisy of urban intersections, and winding dead-ends that seem to always lie in wait for the solitary passerby. If it were up to him, he would build cities according to a new plan whose guiding principles would be lots and lots of sun and wide areas of space.

That's why he also greatly preferred taking walks beyond the city, along boulevards with sparsely-populated homesteads, or else walks in the late afternoon along suburban pastures that vanished gently into never-ending mists . . . .

During this time Odonicz's house underwent radical changes. In keeping with his new-found principles of simplicity and openness, he got rid of anything that could be considered as a cover or a screen.

Therefore, old Persian rugs disappeared, along with Bokharas and Sumaks that muffled the echo of footsteps. From walls came down flowing curtains and drapes. He stripped the windows bare of discreet little curtains, he threw out silk screens. Even a screen of green tassels that had been a favourite of Jadwiga's was no longer allowed to shade with its three-fold wings the interior of the bedroom. Even wardrobes became suspicious pieces of furniture, belonging to the category of hiding-places. Therefore, he had them taken to the attic, making do with ordinary hat-stands and coat-racks.

And so the transformed house acquired a peculiar simplicity. As can be imagined, his few acquaintances commented on the exaggerated primitiveness of his home, mentioning this and that about a hospital-barracks style, but Odonicz, smiling tolerantly, did not take their remarks to heart. On the contrary, with every day he grew more partial to his home, which he left with less and less frequency, avoiding in this manner any surprises waiting for him outside. He liked his quiet, simple rooms where he didn't have to fear any ambush, and where everything was bright and open like the palm of one's hand.

Nothing was hiding behind curtains, nor lurking in the shadows of unnecessary furniture. No romantic dimness or low-lighting existed, nor any shadowy hints or secrets. Everything was evident, like a piece of bread on a plate or a cookbook open on a table.

During the day, the house was bathed in streams of

healthy, robust sunlight; after the first hint of evening twilight, electric light-bulbs blazed. The eyes of the master of the house could freely and with impunity travel across the smooth surface of the walls, not over-hung with drapes, though embellished here and there with a couple of cheerful English prints. Nothing could catch him unawares, nothing could crouch behind some corner without being seen.

'Just as in an open field,' Odonicz frequently thought, taking in the plain surroundings. 'My house is definitely not suitable terrain for any game of hide-and-seek.'

It seemed that these preventive measures achieved their desired result. Odonicz became considerably pacified and even felt relatively happy. And nothing would have spoiled this calm if not for certain funny, as it were, little peculiarities . . . .

One evening Odonicz was struggling for several uninterrupted hours to finish a major scholarly work, which he intended to publish in the near future. The work, which dealt with the natural sciences, criticised certain new biological hypotheses, demonstrating their helplessness before phenomena observed in the life of creatures inhabiting a region between the animal and plant kingdoms.

Wearied by long exertions of thought, Odonicz put aside his pen, lit up a cigarette, after which, straightening his head onto the back of the chair, he placed his right hand on the desk, stretching out his stiff fingers . . . .

Suddenly, he gave a start, for he felt under them something soft and pliant. He drew back his hand involuntarily and glanced attentively at the right part of his desk where a heavy porphyry paperweight usually lay. He discovered, to his amazement, a dry sponge instead of the stone.

He rubbed his eyes and touched the object. It was a sponge! A typical, pale-yellow sponge – *spongia vulgaris* . . . .

'What the devil?' he muttered, turning the object round. 'How did this get here? I don't even use a sponge. Anyway, it's too small to be of any use. Hmm, peculiar . . . . But where, confound it, is that paperweight? It's been in the same place for years.'

And he began to search about the desk, looking in drawers, underneath the table — in vain; the stone had vanished without a trace. In its place lay a sponge, a simple, common sponge .... Was not this an hallucination?

He rose from the table and started to nervously walk about the room.

'Why a sponge?' he asked, perturbed. 'Why exactly a sponge? It could just as well have been a lump of iron or a piece of wood from a fence.'

'With your permission, my dear sir,' suddenly responded some unwelcome inner voice, 'this isn't the same thing. Even such occurrences as these are related. You forget that for several hours you've been dwelling almost exclusively in the world of hydras, sponges, Actiniaria, and Coelenterata. And it was precisely the life of a sponge that most interested you. You won't deny this?'

Odonicz stopped in the middle of the room, struck by this reasoning.

'Hmm, yes,' he muttered, 'sponges did occupy my thoughts for several hours. But so what, damn it?' he suddenly yelled out. 'This still doesn't make sense!'

And he glanced at the desk. But now, to his dumbfounded amazement, he saw, instead of the sponge, the missing paperweight. It was lying quietly and peacefully in its appointed, permanent place, as if nothing had happened. Odonicz swept a hand across his forehead, rubbed his eyes a second time, and convinced himself that he wasn't dreaming: on the desk was lying the paperweight, the porphyritic paperweight with the smooth, rounded knob in its centre. No sign of the sponge — as if it had never been there.

'A delusion,' he declared. 'An hallucination caused by overwork.'

And he returned to his desk. But he couldn't manage to hammer out even one more sentence that night; the 'delusion' gave him no peace, and despite all his efforts, he wasn't able to concentrate on his work ....

The episode of the sponge was a prelude to other similar

manifestations, which from then on began persecuting him with greater frequency. Before long he noticed that other objects in the room would disappear, only to reappear at their familiar place after a while. Conversely, he often discovered on his desk the most varied things that had never been there before.

Yet the most fascinating aspect of this entire situation was that these phenomena arrived concurrently with an interest he had in these objects before their disappearance or emergence. As a general rule he had been thinking intensely about them beforehand.

It was enough for him to think, with a certain dose of inner conviction, that, for example, he had lost some book, to find, a moment later, that it was indeed missing from his library shelf. Similarly, whenever he would clearly imagine the existence of some object on the table, it would soon be there in front of his eyes as if he had summoned it.

These phenomena upset him greatly, giving rise to grave suspicions. Who knew whether this wasn't some new trap? At times he had the feeling that this was yet another attack of 'the unknown,' only from a different side and in a different form. Slowly, certain suggestions and views imposed themselves on him with relentless obsessiveness.

'Does the world which encompasses me exist at all? And if it indeed exists, is it not created by thoughts? Maybe everything is only a fiction of some deeply meditating ego? Somewhere out there in the beyond, someone is constantly, from time immemorial, thinking – and the entire world, and with it the poor little human race, is a product of this perpetual reverie.'

At other times Odonicz fell into an egocentric frenzy and had doubts about the existence of anything but himself. It was only he who continually thought, only he, Dr. Thomas Odonicz, and everything he looked at and perceived was a creation of his mind. Ha! ha! ha! How extraordinary! The world as a product of an individual's thoughts, a mental creation of an insane ego!

The first time he arrived at this conclusion, it weighed

144

heavily on him. Suddenly, in a chill of eerie dread, Odonicz had felt terribly alone.

'And if, indeed, there is nothing beyond the corner? Who can affirm if beyond so-called "reality" anything exists at all? Beyond a reality that I have probably created? As long as I'm steeped in this reality up to my neck, as long as it is sufficient for me – everything is tolerable. But what would happen if I wanted one day to lean out of my safe environment and glance beyond its borders?'

At this point he felt a sharp, deeply piercing chill, a sort of freezing polar atmosphere of eternal night. Before his widening pupils appeared a bloodcurdling vision of a bottomless and boundless emptiness . . . .

Alone he was, completely alone with his thoughts . . . .

One day, shaving before a large hand-held mirror, Odonicz had a strange experience: it suddenly seemed that a part of the room behind him, that part he could see in the mirror, looked somehow different.

He put aside his razor and began to diligently study the reflection of the rear portion of his bedroom. Indeed, for a moment everything behind him looked different. But what that change consisted of, he wasn't able to clearly state. Some specific modification, some strange shift in proportion – something of this sort.

Curious, he put the mirror down on the table and looked around to verify the reality of the situation. But he didn't find anything suspicious: everything was as it used to be.

Calmed, he again looked into the mirror. Now the room seemed normal again; whatever it was had completely disappeared.

'Hyperesthesia of the visual centre, nothing more,' he quietened himself down with the hastily put-together term.

But there were after-effects. From then on Odonicz began to fear what was behind him. And that's why he stopped looking around. If someone were to call out his name on the street, he wouldn't turn around for all the money in the world. Now he also returned home by circuitous ways and never used the same street he initially took. When it was necessary to turn around, he did it with extreme caution and in the slowest possible manner, fearing that by a sudden change in direction he would face that unknown presence. Through slow and gradual movement, he wanted to give it enough time to withdraw or to return to its former innocent posture.

Finally, he pushed this cautiousness to such a degree that whenever he intended looking around, he 'gave prior warning.' Every time he had to leave his desk to go to the back of the room, he first stood up with a noticeably noisy movement of his chair, after which he said in a raised voice, so that he would be clearly heard from behind:

'I am now turning around.'

Only after this announcement, and then waiting a moment more, would he turn in the intended direction.

Life under these conditions soon became torturous. Odonicz, hampered at every step by a thousand fears, every moment potent with danger, led a miserable existence . . .

Yet he became accustomed even to this. Yes, after a while this constant state of strained nerves became second nature to him. The feeling of being surrounded at every moment by mystery, albeit a menacing and dangerous one, cast a gloomy fascination on the grey trial of his life. He gradually grew fond of this game of hide-and-seek; in any event, it seemed more interesting than the banality of people's ordinary experiences. He even developed an appetite for seeking out any sign of strangeness, and it would have been difficult for him to do without the world of enigmas.

Eventually he reduced the doubts which tormented him to this dilemma: Either there is something 'unusual' beyond me, something fundamentally different from that reality which I know as a human being – or else there is nothing, a complete emptiness.

If someone were to ask him which of these two possibilities he would have preferred to meet on the other side,

Odonicz wouldn't have been able to give a definite answer.

Unquestionably, nothingness – absolute, boundless emptiness – would be a horrible thing; on the other hand, maybe nothingness would be better than some frightful reality of another order. For who can know what that other reality really is? And if it is something monstrous, isn't non-existence preferable?

And so a battle started between these two extremes, these two contrary tendencies. On one side he was choked by the iron claws of fear before the unknown, and on the other side he was propelled by a tragic curiosity into the arms of the daily-growing mystery. Some kind of wary, wise voice warned him against making a dangerous decision, but Odonicz dismissed this advice with an indulgent smile. The enticing daemon lured him ever closer with its siren promises . . . .

Until finally he succumbed . . . .

One autumn evening, sitting before an open book, he suddenly sensed behind his shoulders the presence of that mystery. Something was happening behind him: secret wings were parting, curtains were being lifted up, drapes were being drawn apart . . . .

And then a crazy desire arose within him – to turn around and glance at what was behind him, just this time, this one and only time. It would be enough to turn his head without giving the usual warning, so that he could surprise it before it got a chance to run away – one cast of the eye would be enough, one short, momentary glance . . . .

Odonicz dared this glance. With a movement as quick as lightning, he spun around to see what was behind him. And then from his lips came an inhuman cry of boundless alarm and terror; he convulsively grabbed at his heart and, as if struck by a thunderbolt, fell lifeless to the bare floor.

AFTERWORD

THE AREA – A CONTEMPORARY HORROR STORY?

A young girl lies in bed drawing in a notebook she has been given. She is ill and her mind is over-active. She draws a house and puts herself in one of the upper rooms. Every day she adds on a little more, roughly and crookedly drawn, a child's first attempts. An innocent pastime. But at night the house comes back to haunt her in dreams. The house and grounds are changed into a nightmare world from which she can't escape. The drawings she has created from a tortured imagination become objects of a terrifying propensity. The most frightening aspect of the whole situation becomes evident – she cannot escape from her own mind.

This scenario is drawn from a modern children's book. We turn back a hundred years to Grabinski's 'The Area.' The writer Wrzesmian stops writing, completely stops. His hitherto 'original, insanely strange works' cease to be produced. Now begins the process of withdrawal from the world, one which is a natural consequence of being a writer but one which Wrzesmian makes complete and absolute. For him, the artist's constant struggle between solitude and living in society has been fought and decided. From now on his own mind is his only inspiration, his weird imaginings the impetus he needs for the creation of his art.

Writing, however, is no longer the ultimate aim. He craves a freedom of expression that extends beyond the written word, the limitations of language. He desires to go further than any artist has been before, to change fiction into reality, to give his thoughts and dreams an actual substance which has been hitherto denied them.

Like the girl in the story, Wrzesmian's frustrated longings become focused on a house. This house, although situated across the street from him, is as much a product of his mind as the child's pencil drawing. It is described in a wealth of gloomy and sensuous detail, casting a spell as if it has been sleeping for one hundred years – 'At the end of a black double row of cypresses, their two lines containing a stone pathway, appeared a several stepped terrace where a weighty, stylized double door let to the interior – Only two eternal fountains quietly wept, shedding water from marble basins onto clusters of rich, red roses'. The house and gardens are dormant but ominous and waiting. Like Wrzesmian's mind, which critics and the public have dismissed as spent and prematurely depleted, they are ostensibly inactive but underneath are seething with unimaginable horror.

Only 'unimaginable', however, in the context of the reality which we encounter every day. The mind however contains horrors and thoughts which are rarely articulated and seldom brought to light. But, 'From underneath the garden, treacherously concealed humidity crawled out here and there with dark oozing' and very soon Wrzesmian begins to see the face of a man at the window which seizes him with 'a vague dread'. The house is becoming active, given life by Wrzesmian's own mind.

The horror of having one's innermost imaginings turned into a form of reality becomes increasingly obvious as the drama draws to its inevitable and terrifying conclusion. Like the child, Wrzesmian discovers that it is impossible to escape the horror because this horror is within him and yet now also external. The terror which grips him is our terror at having our own worst thoughts brought to light and acting upon us. They are unstoppable because they are propelled by the force of the mind and they are intolerable because they are a product of the darkest part of ourselves.

This is perhaps the secret of popularity of horror books and films. We can explore the inner recesses of the mind and yet can walk away from it. Most recently, Clive Barker in his 'Hellraiser' films has also used this 'Grabinski' technique – just twist the box and your most dread thoughts become reality, you might think you can control them but they are now independent of your mind, the pain and torture you only vaguely imagined are now standing before you. Like Wrzesmian, the only possible end is annihilation because the self cannot be divided. The mind is now all powerful and cannot be denied –

'We want full life! You confined us to this house, you wretch! We want to go out into the world; we want to be released from this place to live in freedom! Your blood will fortify us, your blood will give us strength! Strangle him! Strangle him!'

For Grabinski, it is the mind which is his main concern. His perception of the force and inner recesses of the mind dominates his work. The inner thoughts take substance and become the outer reality, often with horrifying consequences. It is this which makes his stories so disturbing because they are a journey into our own 'Dark Domain'.

The Dedalus Book of Polish Fantasy – edited and translated by Wiesiek Powaga

Poland's strong Catholic faith engendered in its literature a lively awareness of the Devil and a love of the supernatural. The Devil is a leading figure in Polish fantastic literature, and we see him in many different roles and guises: from the personification of pure malice to a pitiful, unfortunate individual and even a patriotic hero. The centuries of familiarity with this unearthly power resulted in a rich story-telling tradition centred on what was strange, mysterious and magical.

The Dedalus Book of Polish Fantasy offers the best of this tradition, which began with the early Romantics, who first started collecting folk-tales and legends, re-working their themes to produce such classics as Barszczewski's *Head Full of Screaming Hair* and Potocki's *The Saragossa Manuscript*.

The next great flowering of Polish fantastic fiction occurred at the beginning of the twentieth century with the stories of T. Micinski and, more particularly, Stefan Grabinski, whose genius gave it a new dimension.

The writings of Bruno Schultz and Witold Gombrowicz, and lesser known contemporary authors like Andrei Szczypiorski and Wiktor Worofzylski, show that literary fantasy is still a fertile and thriving part of Polish fiction.

Most of the stories in *The Dedalus Book of Polish Fantasy* appear in English for the first time.

£8.99   ISBN 1 873982 90 9   320p paperback original

The Dedalus Book of Austrian Fantasy – editor Mike Mitchell

'Subtitled "*The Meyrink Years 1890–1930*", this is a superb collection of the bizarre, the terrifying and the twisted, as interpreted by the decadents and obsessives of *fin de siècle* Vienna. It features big names like Kafka, Rilke and Schnitzler, but more intriguing are the lesser-known writers such as Franz Theodor Csokor with the vampiric "*The Kiss of the Stone Woman*", Karl Hans Strobl, whose "*The Wicked Nun*" begins as a ghost story but twists and turns into insanity and Paul Busson, contributing an uncanny tale of feminine sorcery, "*Folter's Gems!*"'

Time Out

'Divided into five sections (Possessed Souls, Dream and Nightmare, Death, The Macabre, Satire) that tell you all you need to know, the stand out works are those of Gustav Meyrink, Strobl and Schnitzler and Franz Csokor's wonderful, mad chiller "*The Kiss of the Stone Woman*".

The best stories faultlessly follow the traditional template of deepening mystery grafted onto time-honoured methods of signalling narrative action. Recommended'

City Limits

£8.99   ISBN 0 946626 93 6 416pp   B Format